I0628520

THE AMAZING
MARTIN BRETT

Ernest Dudley, the creator of the famous criminolo-gist Dr. Morelle, here gives us four stories of another brilliant detective, whom the newspapers have dubbed "The Amazing Martin Brett."

Martin Brett appears to be selfish and lazy, and his effort in solving crimes is entirely motivated by the size of his fee. His attractive secretary is often the butt of his sardonic humour and sexist remarks, which she finds unnecessary and uncalled for. But she puts up with him because she suspects Brett has a secret sorrow, some woman in his past...and as a detective, he *always* solves his cases!

Borgo Press Books by ERNEST DUDLEY

The Amazing Martin Brett: Classic Crime Stories
Department of Spooks: Stories of Suspense and Mystery
Dr. Morelle Investigates: Two Classic Crime Tales
Dr. Morelle Meets Murder: Classic Crime Stories
New Cases for Dr. Morelle: Classic Crime Stories
The Return of Sherlock Holmes: A Classic Crime Tale

THE AMAZING MARTIN BRETT

CLASSIC CRIME STORIES

ERNEST DUDLEY

THE BORGO PRESS

MMXII

THE AMAZING MARTIN BRETT

Copyright © 2012 by Susan Dudley-Allen

FIRST EDITION

Published by Wildside Press LLC

www.wildsidebooks.com

DEDICATION

For Susan Dudley-Allen

CONTENTS

THE CASE OF THE BURIED HATCHET

I opened the door with MARTIN BRETT on the frosted-glass panel and went in. He was standing by the window looking down at the street, and as I crossed over I caught a glimpse below of the tall, plump figure that was Farringdon Tisdall get into a sleek limousine and drive off. The great financier had just left after half-an-hour's interview with Mr. Brett, and the aroma of cigar hung expensively all over the office. He had also left a retaining-fee of mouth-watering magnitude, his personal cheque for which I placed on the desk.

"What it must be like to be filthy rich," I said. I was thinking of how the money could set me up cosily in the way of frothy frillies and other girlish fancies.

"They tell me you can still sleep badly for all the cash in Farringdon Tindall's coffers," Mr. Brett said over his shoulder.

I said: "If you had that amount to spend, who'd worry about wasting time in bed."

Still without turning his gaze from the direction the car had gone, Mr. Brett said; "Perhaps you'll be intrigued to know you won't be climbing into your cot early tonight, anyway."

Which brought from me a look of interest plus surprise, plus slight apprehension. What job were we going on this time after office-hours? I said: "Mr. Brett? Someone we know throwing a party?"

He came away from the window, moved slowly to his desk, tapped the ash off his cigarette. "Farringdon Tisdall is," he said. "We're invited."

"How awfully jolly of him," I said as casually as I could. Though, of course, I was rather thrilled. I'd got a cunning little white number I hadn't worn since I bought it, and this promised to be the sort of occasion where it should be put to the test. There'd be a really smart crowd there, I knew. I'd heard of the kind of parties Farringdon Tisdall put on. Everything regardless. But inside that new gown and a hair-do—if my hairdresser could fit it in—I felt I could cope. I asked:

"What are we there for, to keep an eye on the silver?"

He handed me a small piece of paper. It had been torn from an ordinary writing pad and on it were gummed in letters cut from a newspaper:

'DEAR SIR—SOMEONE WILL BE AFTER
THE CRIMSON LAKE TONIGHT. THIS IS
A WARNING FROM A
WELL-WISHER.'

Mr. Brett explained; "The Crimson Lake is a ruby, quite an expensive piece." He nodded towards the bit of paper. "He received it this morning."

"Has he got anyone in mind?"

"Nobody in particular. But after he brushed off my suggestion, mightn't it merely be a hoax, he pointed out there'll be two or three hundred guests stamping around tonight. Among them possibly one who simply can't wait to get his hands on the ruby."

"I should have thought if he'd locked the thing away somewhere good and safe, he'd have nothing to worry about."

He eyed the tip of his cigarette and said slowly: "That did occur to me, too."

There was a faintly derisive note in his voice, which made me glance at him sharply. But he only grinned at me enigmatically and bunged into the chair and put his feet up on the desk. I studied the warning message again in case I'd missed anything significant about it. I noticed the letters were neatly cut out and showed up with a pinkish edge to them against the white paper on which they'd been gummed. Nothing startling in all that though, and I looked inquiringly at Mr. Brett. His long face was as full of expression as a poker-playing mandarin—if mandarins play poker, which is something I've never asked about.

"I'm a girl of simple ideas," I shrugged. "So whatever it is goes on, goes on way over my head."

"I didn't say anything."

"It's what you're thinking."

"Something tells me you evidently suspect more in this than meets the eye." He indicated Farringdon Tisdall's cheque. "Personally, only thing of any importance meets *my* eye is that. Which offers me the greatest inducement, so far, for taking on the job." He paused. "And yet somehow, Beautiful," he went on—and I gave him the chill stare I always handed him when he used that familiar tone with me—"I'm getting the idea there night be another interesting attraction to the case after all. Apart from this," picking up the cheque and carefully putting it in his wallet.

I didn't get his drift at all. But something had caused him to reach the conclusion he was going to have to work harder on the job this evening than merely prop up Farringdon Tisdell's buffet-bar. I had the smart idea the cheque had something to do with it. I'd never known him act like that over one before, tucking it away as if it were a vital clue or something. Always cheques were just put aside until I paid them into his account in the routine way. But this one was obviously more important than that. How or why exactly I couldn't guess, so I waited for him to tell me more.

His eyes were narrowed as he said: "I'll need all the dope on Tisdall pronto. Bill Foster will fix you up. You'll have to see him personally, so better organize it soon's you had your lunch."

"Yes, Mr. Brett." I glanced at my wristwatch. "If that'll be all for now, I'll start moving. It's about time to put on the nose-bag."

He nodded. "Dig up everything you can from the Tisdall files, and flutter your long eyelashes at Bill. When it comes to knowing the inside stuff on people, his big ear's closer to the ground than anyone in Fleet Street. Especially if it's dirty ground."

I resented his suggestion as being uncalled for, and unnecessary I switched on the old eye-work business with men. After all, I can't help it if my eyelashes *are* long. But Mr. Brett always likes to get in a dig at my face or figure, just because I don't happen to look like the back of a cab, and my curves happen in the right places. As I've probably mentioned before, I have the notion he sounds off that way on account of some secret sorrow, some woman in his past. Which is a pity; plenty fall for him who could help him forget that yesterday's memory if he'd give them the chance. But all they ever get from him is the sort of encouragement you'd give a cobra without its fangs drawn.

However, I just pretended not to notice he'd said anything I didn't like, and said: "I gather you think Mr. Tisdall may have a skeleton in his cupboard?"

"Now you come to mention it," he said, "I fancy I did catch the echo of something rattling back of his mind during our little chat. Or it may only have been the mice."

And with a sardonic grin Mr. Brett stubbed out his cigarette and left it at that. I manhandled a sandwich and two cups of coffee at a cafeteria and grabbed a taxi for Fleet Street. As I paid it off outside the *Daily Courier* office, I was just in time to catch Bill Foster coming through the swing doors. He was looking bigger and untidier than ever and whooped like a Red Indian when he saw me. He was going for a drink and a bite, but when I told him what I was after, he took my arm in his dear old breezy way and we went up in the lift to the newsroom. It was pretty quiet as newsrooms went, and I parked myself on my desk and smiled graciously at a passing copy-boy who ogled my legs, while Bill got me the file on Farringdon Tisdall.

It was a fat file, all right. Tisdall had stamped his dynamic personality on the world of finance in no uncertain way. With the cuttings on his meteoric business career went all the trimmings of his social climb. His yacht, his racing-stable, his country houses, villa on the Mediterranean, all the rest. Plenty about the Blue Lake Sapphire too. While I was working my way through it, scribbling notes of any stuff that looked particularly interesting for Mr. Brett, Bill ambled off and returned with another file, which he slapped down beside the other.

He watched my face as I stared at It, a bit puzzled. The name on the file was LYDIA DELMAR. Which didn't mean anything to me at all. Except made me think of a name for some ice cream or something.

"Getting your names a bit mixed, Bill, aren't you?" I said.

He shook his head, his smile broader.

"You want the inside stuff as well, you said."

I tapped the Delmar file. "But where does she—?"

"He was nuts about her," Bill said.

Lydia Delmar's press-clippings were mostly photographs. Photos of an extremely delectable-looking blonde. The earlier captions underneath told you she was the well-known mannequin, and I began to remember I'd seen her in the smart fashion magazines.

Then came some later photos of her smiling dreamily at a nice-looking dark young man with a sprinkle of confetti around his ears. The captions included his name, Raymond Ward. Bill Foster jabbed at him with his pipe-stem.

"He *used* to be Tisdall's private secretary."

"Like that was it?" I said.

"Like that," Bill said. "Chucked the big man, she did, for the other one."

"What's happened to them now?"

"Lydia's in New York working for some advertising firm, I believe. The boy's still around London, trying to scrape enough money to go out and join her."

"Not much of a marriage, that."

"Oh, I expect they write each other. Often think marriages would work out better if the husband lived in one country and the wife in another."

"You have the dearest ideas," I told him.

He grinned back at me. Then he said reflectively. "It knocked Tisdall all of a doodah. Some say he's never forgiven either of 'em. Hardly credit it, eh? Fact. All that dough, power couldn't buy him that little doll." He jabbed Lydia Delmar's photo with his pipe. "'Course, Tisdall kicked out young Ward on the spot. Real vicious, he was. S'pose it hit his pride and all that."

"Quite the dramatic stuff," I said, taking a cigarette from my case. Bill held a match to it, then applied it to his pipe. He puffed away thoughtfully for a moment, until the match he'd forgotten to blow out burned his fingers. Idly he turned some of the cuttings from the big file and picked out a photo of Tisdall.

"Talking of dramatics," he said slowly, "I always have the feeling one of these days I'll see that dial over a caption of quite a different kind."

I looked at him curiously. "How different?"

"I dunno," he muttered. "Something—*unpleasant.*"

I studied the face again with fresh interest. It wasn't a nice face, I thought, and remembered that was the reaction I had when he'd come into the office that morning. It was puffy and the eyes were small and lidless. But staring at it now, it didn't give me any reason to guess just how soon Bill Foster's prophetic words would be coming home like birds of ill-omen to roost.

When I got back, Mr. Brett was in, looking very much the same as when I'd left him, with his feet still up on the desk. Just as if he'd never been out of the office. Automatically I expected to see the whisky-bottle at his elbow—he often stayed behind and took his lunch from that. But it was nowhere around. Instead, there were several newspapers draped over everything, which weren't there before, so I knew he had in fact been out. I looked in again presently with the Farringdon Tisdall dope, and he was staring at the anonymous message through a magnifying glass. Apparently he was comparing it with something in one of the newspapers. Then I noticed ail the papers were financial sheets. *The Financial Market, Daily Finance,* and so on.

After a while it seemed to sink in I was in the same room with him, and he turned and gave me a grin.

"How's it feel to watch the Great Sleuth at work?" He said, with that sarcastic jeer which was his own particular brand. "Give you a thrill?"

"From where I'm standing, you look more like someone playing the Stock Market, in a crazy sort of way," I said. "Here's the stuff on Farringdon Tisdall."

And I went back to my office to get on with the job of dealing with the mailing, the filing—the routine stuff which Mr. Brett apparently fondly imagines is done by a troupe of tender-hearted pixies after I've locked up for the day.

After a while the speaking-machine on my desk crackled, and his voice came at me like water sizzling over hot coals. "Leave your lipstick and compact for now, Gorgeous, you're wanted."

"Yes, Mr. Brett," I said back into the box even more icily if possible than ever, and pulling a face at the darned thing. It *would* happen his jibe in the dark would catch me coincidentally just at the moment I'd paused to fix my make-up. I made an irritable grab for my notebook and went on in. He was by the window moodily contemplating the street. On a chair beside him was one of the newspapers, the warning letter, and the magnifying glass. He turned to me and passed on the newspaper, which was of a pinky shade.

"Take a look at that."

I saw at once part of a column he'd marked off with pencil. I puzzled at it, doing my best to appear as if it was making sense. Seemingly it was an extract from some company report, jam full of technical terms and references whose meaning was clear to me as mud. If it had been written in Aztec, it couldn't have told me more.

"Very interesting," I said.

"If you find that improving to the mind," he grinned, "this should kill you." And handed me the letter. "Take a peek at it, through this," giving me the glass.

And then, *bingo!* I got what he was getting at.

The letters forming the warning message had obviously been cut out from an issue of the newspaper I'd just been looking at. Comparison proved that the type was identical with that of the pencilled column. Under the magnifying glass, the pink edge I'd only half-noticed earlier on round each letter so neatly gummed to the writing paper was the exact shade of the newssheet.

Mr. Brett saw by my face that the penny had dropped. "Came a great light," he murmured sardonically:

"And what does it add up to?" I said.

He lit a cigarette and idly watched a puff of smoke curl ceilingwards, before he said slowly:

"It adds up to the possibility that the sender of the note warning Farringdon Tisdall his pet ruby was in danger of being pinched was himself a reader of the financial press. From which hypothesis—" Mr. Brett cleared his larynx and his manner became almost expansive, sure sign he was beginning to enjoy listening to the sound of his own voice, "—could evolve a logical sequence of questions. For example, what persons most interested in the ruby are also interested followers of newspapers devoted solely to finance? Having answered that one, you could by a narrowing-down process proceed inevitably to put your finger on the party who sent the letter."

"And when will you be taking *that* rabbit out of the hat?" I said. He regarded me with that derisive grin of his through another cloud of cigarette smoke.

"I'll do nay utmost, Dream Girl," he said, "to show you the trick tonight."

* * * * * *

Farringdon Tisdall's house in Highgate was a whacking great white mansion place standing in its own grounds screened from the road by trees, with a wide drive curving up to it. Mr. Brett didn't habitually claim the power of sixth sense, but on this occasion he seemed to have the idea nothing sensational would happen at the party before we appeared, so on our arrival the drive was already packed with opulent-looking cars, and I caught the sound of a dance-orchestra giving out as we went. up the steps.

Coming back to the hall to find Mr. Brett after dumping my cape, I caught sight of a face that made me stop in my tracks. I'm pretty good at recognizing people and it was him all right. I must have been staring pretty hard. Anyhow he turned his head and stared back, finally giving me a tentative half-smile. I didn't reciprocate, however, not with the idea of snubbing him, but because I was too preoccupied. I hurried on my way and found Mr. Brett standing somewhat aloof from the crowd milling round.

"Guess who I've just seen?" I said a trifle breathlessly.

"I'll buy it. Who?"

"Raymond Ward, the ex-secretary who pinched his girlfriend. Remember?" Well, not unnaturally I expected him to show some sign of surprise or even a mild interest, but all he did was to go a little bleak round the mouth and gaze past my left ear with a faraway expression.

"Wonder which way the bar is?" he said.

But before he could make a move, a character with receding hair had come up and eyed him expectantly.

"Mr. Martin Brett?"

Mr. Brett nodded.

"My name is Selby. Mr. Tisdall's secretary."

"Good," Mr. Brett said, without any enthusiasm whatsoever.

Farringdon Tisdall had certainly taken no chances over the man he'd hired to take the place of young Ward.

Selby was a weedy-looking individual with thick-lensed spectacles and about as much appeal as a jellyfish.

I calculated there was practically no risk at all of him running off with anybody's girlfriend, except maybe another jellyfish. And she'd have to be frantically hard up. He coughed apologetically, looked as if he was washing his hands without any soap, and said;

"Mr. Tisdall asked me to look out for you soon as

you arrived. He would like to see you in the library."

Mr. Brett said abruptly: "Has he got any drink there?"

The secretary looked slightly startled, but recovered himself to smile thinly. "I'm sure Mr. Tisdall will be able to offer you some refreshment."

Mr. Brett threw him a nod and we trailed off to the library. Farringdon Tisdall greeted us with quite a show of affability, and with a cigar which looked about three feet long stuck in his face, began pouring out the drinks. As he handed them to us, he said:

"I thought we might have a chat and if there's anything you'd like to know that would be useful...." He left the rest of the sentence suspended on the cigar smoke and looked helpful.

Mr. Brett let his gaze take in the surroundings over the rum of his glass. And Farringdon Tisdall's library was something that you really had to take in. Luxury literally leered at you from every side. Rich oak panelling from floor to ceiling, curtains and tapestries that glowed with gorgeous colour, and a carpet so thick you felt you were walking in velvet up to your ankles,

After a moment Mr. Brett said: "Where's the ruby tucked away?"

The other crossed obediently to the wide fireplace, and then pressed somewhere underneath the massive ornately carved mantelpiece. At his touch a section of the woodwork about nine inches square sprang open to reveal a small wall safe. "Neat isn't it?" Mr. Tisdall said over his shoulder. He went on; "Needless to say, we in this room are the only people who know if its existence."

Mr. Brett glanced casually at Selby who'd remained unobtrusively in the background, making no contribution to the conversation, and doing precious little to improve the scenery either. Now, however, he ventured to put his oar in with:

"*And* my predecessor."

"Ah, yes," Farringdon Tisdall murmured as if reminded of the fact. His face took on an abstract expression, then he seemed to dismiss whatever it was he'd been thinking, and bent slightly in an attitude of concentration before the safe.

There was a sharp metallic click and the safe-door swung back. Mr. Tisdall rummaged inside and after a moment held the Crimson Lake under the light for our inspection. It was beautiful, glowing up at us like something alive. I cooed the usual assortment of appropriately admiring remarks while Mr. Brett, his thoughts for all I knew wandering round the wilds of Tibet or somewhere, gazed at it as if it was a bit of coloured glass.

Then Farringdon Tisdall looked up and said conversationally: "By the way, Mr. Selby's—er—predecessor already referred to happens to be one of my guests tonight." He smiled slowly. but it seemed to me it didn't quite match up with his lidless eyes. "Yes," he went on smoothly, "the circumstances of his leaving were somewhat painful to me at the time, but I hope all that's forgotten now. And forgiven. His presence here is in fact an attempt on my part to persuade him to let bygones be bygones. Ward his name is, Raymond Ward. Charming and very able young man." He considered a moment while Mr. Brett and I didn't bat an eyelash, though what we were hearing hardly added up to the inside-story tipped off to me by Bill Foster. Mr. Tisdall was continuing: "I feel I was perhaps too harsh on him. After all, one shouldn't forget the time when one's self was young—" He broke off and turned to Selby: "Mr. Ward has arrived?"

"Er—yes," the other nodded.

"Perhaps you'd find him presently and say I'd be glad for him to join me over a drink?"

"Very well." He hesitated for a moment and then muttered: "If you'll excuse me, there are one or two other matters I have to attend to."

After he'd gone, Mr, Brett said: "Presumably your secretary has some idea why we're here?"

"He knows who you are, yes. No one else does, of course."

"And the letter?"

"I told him about that—I saw no reason why I shouldn't. Why?"

"No reason at all," Mr. Brett agreed amiably.

He began to wander apparently aimlessly round the room drawing abstractedly at his cigarette. I had worn out all the superlatives I could think up over the ruby, and there was a little silence. Mr. Tisdall glanced at Mr. Brett over his cigar, shot a glance of inquiry at me, which I answered with a beaming smile, leaving him to make what he liked of it, and he crossed over to the safe with the ruby. As he bent to close it up, he said over his shoulder: "Of course, as an added precaution I switch the combination every two or three days. Only Selby and I know what it is."

The remark was intended for Mr. Brett, who, however, appeared to have lost what little interest he'd ever had in the jewel and was, I saw from the corner of my eye glancing idly through some magazines and newspapers on a table. I covered up his unresponsiveness by blathering something about what a smart idea it was for Mr. Tisdall to take the extra precaution.

And then Mr. Brett spoke from the other side of the room, very quietly. "No risk of either of you jotting down the combination and leaving it about for anyone else to see?" he asked, which just shows what a mistake it is to kid yourself he ever lets a darn thing get past him, no matter how much you think his mind's on something else at the time.

The other replied that the combination was simple enough to remember, no need to write it down, you just kept it in your head. A few minutes later we left Farringdon Tisdall in the library, and Mr. Brett complaining he was still thirsty, was pushing off in the direction of what he hoped was a bar. On our way we saw Selby talking to Raymond Ward, and they passed us, presumably going to the library. The secretary peered at us shortsightedly with a nod of acknowledgement, while the other looked at me as if he'd liked to give me that tentative half-smile again.

Mr. Brett leant against the bar for a surprisingly short time and I trailed after him back to the hall. He lit a cigarette for me, then his own, and I listened to the dance-music watching the celebrities, and those who thought they were, passing to and fro, while he fixed his eyes in a basilisk stare on the passage leading to the library. Presently he relaxed somewhat and Raymond Ward appeared.

Mr. Brett went purposefully over to him.

"Mr. Ward?"

The other said; "Yes," saw me, and definitely brightened. Mr. Brett cut out the fancy work, said straight away who he was.

"Think a quiet little chat is indicated," he said, while Ward was recovering from his surprise, and led the way over to a secluded corner behind the wide staircase. There was a sudden air of urgency about him which made me give him a sideways glance.

"First," he said briskly, "hasn't it struck you as slightly incongruous your being here tonight?"

Ward caught the unmistakable implication behind the question. "You mean him inviting me—of all people?" And went on: "Well he phoned and said he was prepared to forget what happened, let bygones be bygones and all that, if I felt the same way about it. *He* wanted to bury the hatchet, he said, and would I come to this party and we'd shake hands over a drink. So—well—I don't go in for bearing malice and here I am."

"You didn't think this idea might be to bury the hatchet in you?" Mr. Brett said, and the other looked at him sharply.

"What d'you mean?"

"Never mind," Mr. Brett waved the idea aside. "So you've been having a drink and Farringdon Tisdall's been magnanimous all over the library. Quite like old times, eh?"

Ward grinned. "Roughly that," he said. "He asked after Lydia—my wife you know." He hesitated and said: "He and Lydia were—"

"I know," cut in Mr. Brett.

"Matter of fact, it *was* quite like old times." And he laughed, as if something had amused him. "He even asked me to show him an old handkerchief trick that used to peeve him because he could never do it."

"What handkerchief trick?"

"Tie it so it looks like a rabbit. He always made a hash of it. Even when he tried it just now."

I noticed the handkerchief protruding from his breast pocket looked a little crumpled.

Mr. Brett's face suddenly froze. Then:

"I'm interested in tricks," he said softly. "Show."

Raymond Ward smiled and proceeded to oblige. As he pulled the handkerchief out something slipped from its folds and lay in the palm of his hand. He stared at it stupidly.

"Some trick," murmured Mr. Brett as the Crimson Lake ruby gleamed up at us. He grabbed it. "Wait here," he snapped at the other, who was still glassy-eyed as if he'd been kicked smartly in the stomach by a recalcitrant mule, and was gone.

I managed to catch up with him as he reached the library and followed him in, to be brought up with a sickening shock. Farringdon Tisdall hadn't in my opinion made a particularly pretty picture before, but now slumped over his writing desk with his head bashed in, he was a ghastly sight. Mr. Brett had already crossed to him.

"Is he dead?" I asked, my voice sounding as if it belonged to someone else.

He nodded grimly, glanced at a hefty-looking ornament—which could have done the job—sprawled on the desk amongst scattered papers and capsized inkstand from which green ink had spilled and was staining the gorgeous carpet. He jabbed a bell push, and then I followed his look across to where the wall safe gaped wide-open. My brain was spinning round in crazy circles as I tried to make sense of what must have happened. It seemed fantastic to believe Raymond Ward could have done this terrible thing, yet— My bewilderment was momentarily interrupted as Selby hurried into the room. He stared unbelievingly at the figure at the desk, then swayed and seemed as if he was about to collapse, only Mr. Brett brought him up with a jerk.

"Get the police," he said curtly.

"But—but a doctor?" the secretary gasped as he moved like a sleepwalker to the phone.

"Needn't worry about that for the moment. Police."

Selby mumbled incoherently and lifted the receiver. Mr. Brett stared across at him through a puff of cigarette smoke and said slowly: "I'll talk to 'em. *And you'd better make it good.*"

My heart seemed to stop in that dreadful silence as Selby blinked over the receiver and mouthed: "What—what d'you mean?"

"Only you knew that combination beside Tisdall. Trouble was, when you opened the safe you were too late. He'd already planted it on young Ward." He thrust his hand into his pocket and brought out the Crimson Lake. "That's what you were after, wasn't it?"

Selby's face was drained putty-colour. "I—I haven't been in here since Ward," he rasped.

"That won't do either," Mr. Brett smiled bleakly. "Look at your shirt cuff."

The other sucked in his breath and peered short-sightedly at his hand clutching the phone. *The cuff showing above it was stained with ink bright green.*

* * * * * * *

"Of course," said Mr. Brett in the taxi later, "Selby planned the whole thing with the idea suspicion would fall on Ward. The mere fact Ward hadn't the ruby on him wouldn't necessarily clear him—police could argue he'd hidden it to collect later. But what Selby didn't know was Tisdall had invited his ex-secretary for sole purpose of planting the ruby on him, then accusing him of theft."

"Motive: revenge?"

"Just that. Tisdall himself concocted an anonymous warning as excuse to have me on the spot when his scheme went into operation. I confirmed my earlier hunch on that score when I took a peek at his papers in the library. Remember the financial sheet, type identical with gummed letters of note? Tisdall had an issue of that paper, with bits cut out of it."

I murmured something appropriately appreciative of Mr. Brett's talents. Mr. Brett, who was beginning to wallow in the sounds from his own vocal chords again, went on: "He planted the stone when Ward was doing his handkerchief trick. Selby, the moment the boy goes, pops into library, socks Tisdall, and then discovers he's done the dirty deed for nothing. No ruby. So he beats it. The rest...." And he allowed the rest to melt into cigarette smoke.

I remembered something. "What about your cheque?" I asked. "Now Farringdon Tisdall's no longer with us?"

Mr. Brett smiled at me derisively from the darkness of the taxi. "Cashed it this morning. When I went out to get the papers. Just an idea I had something inconvenient might happen to my client."

THE CASE OF THE
BORGIA RELIC

"Mr. Martin Brett's office," I said automatically as I lifted the receiver,

"My name is Gale, Edwin Gale." The voice over the wire had a pleasing resonance. "I wonder when is the earliest I could see Mr. Brett? It's pretty urgent, I'm afraid," a note of anxiety edging his tone.

"He's awfully busy," I said dubiously, cocking an eye towards the half-open door which had MARTIN BRETT on the frosted-glass panel—and beyond where Mr. Brett was tilted back in a chair his feet on the desk, idly blowing smoke-rings at the ceiling.

"Couldn't he possibly fit me in this afternoon?" the other urged. "I—er—that is, I think I could make it worth his while."

I made my voice sound as if I was wearing a slightly bored smile. "That would hardly influence Mr. Brett if his appointment diary is already full," I purred.

He was suitably impressed—they always were when I gave 'em that line—and quickly tried to cover up his clumsy attempt at persuasion. "Quite, quite," he jerked out. "What I mean is—well—I need his help quickly, or it'll be too late. And if there was some way in which he *could* manage to—that is—well, I really am in a hellish fix—"

I interrupted his floundering. "Will you hold on a moment, please, Mr. Gale? I'll just see if there is a chance—"

"I'd be most grateful," he said, brightening. "Any time this afternoon—"

I left the receiver on my desk and went into Mr. Brett, closing the door after me. "A Mr. Gale on the phone with something on his mind," I told him.

He didn't take the slightest notice, just puffed another smoke-ring and watched it rise with somewhat morose concentration. He hadn't been in the best of moods all morning. Maybe it was because he was a little edgy on account of an arduous and extremely tricky case he'd been working on and just cleared up after a painstakingly involved investigation: This private detective business isn't all fun and games with a neat, dramatically clean-cut climax by a long chalk. Too often it's a sordid, wearing racket and dirty all the way through. And even though the fee was a fat one, I knew Mr. Brett hadn't enjoyed this last little job at all. Or again, maybe it wasn't that either. Maybe he'd just been reminded, for some reason that I wouldn't know about, of that secret sorrow of his. I've mentioned it before, my intuition that there's been some woman in his past.

Anyway, I said patiently: "He wants to know if you'll see him this afternoon. Sounds pretty het-up, if you ask me."

He said without turning his head: "I'd be more interested to know what sort of a sound his cheque will make."

"I think he's the kind that talks money," I said. (As I believe I've also mentioned before, Mr. Brett runs his business on strictly business lines, none of the amateur gumshoe who snoops round outsmarting the police just for the hell of it about him. And if that doesn't sound so glamorous as those clever-clever sleuths you read about in books, that's too bad.)

Mr. Brett gave me his saturnine smile, "All right," he said, "if you say so."

"Three this afternoon?"

He nodded.

"Yes, Mr. Brett," I said and went out. I picked up the phone and cooed: "So sorry to keep you waiting, Mr. Gale—"

"Oh, that's all right. Have you managed to fix anything?"

"I've had a word with Mr. Brett, and he finds he could see you at three o'clock this afternoon."

"Splendid, splendid. I really am most awfully grateful to him. Three o'clock? I'll be there on the dot. And again, thank you very, very much."

Mr. Gale arrived at five minutes to three and outwardly, at any rate, confirmed the impression he'd given me over the phone he was the type who talked money. He was middle-aged plump and immaculately dressed in astrakhan-collared coat and black Homburg. Of course, I'm not mug enough to be fooled just by the way a prospective client is dolled up; an astrakhan coat can hide an empty tummy and an even emptier bank-account, I know. But Edwin Gale looked to me as if besides his opulent exterior his pockets were very nicely lined, too.

He gave me a charming smile when I asked him to park himself, that Mr. Brett would be free in a moment; and produced a gilt and cream box from his pocket which he handed to me. My heart fairly bounced with excitement as I opened it and goggled at the ornately carved bottle of perfume inside. It was quite the most wildly expensive stuff I'd ever seen at such close quarters. He was saying:

"Your voice seemed to tell me somehow yours was the personality that particular perfume would suit, And," with a glance that was meant to be veiled but which I could read like a book, "I'm not disappointed. I hope you aren't either?"

"It's very kind of you," I said.

"Merely a slight repayment of your kindness to me this morning," he murmured. "I need Mr, Brett's aid quite desperately." His face clouded for a moment. Then he smiled, again and with a nod to towards the gift said: "I hope you'll accept it—that is, unless your mother has absolutely forbidden you to take presents from strange men?"

I laughed in what I hoped was a delightful way. "My mother never said anything about such a lovely present as this," I said, removing the stopper and breathing in deeply. He was laughing, too, and then the speaking-machine on my desk clicked alive and Mr. Brett's sardonically familiar tones crackled at me.

"When you're through laughing at Mr. Gale's funny stories, Gorgeous, perhaps you'll show the gentleman in."

"Yes. Mr. Brett," I said, with all the icy hauteur I could freeze into my voice. I turned to Mr. Gale, who was looking at me with raised eyebrows, and flashed him my most radiant smile, "Mr. Brett will see you now."

Mr. Brett told me to stay and take notes while he waved the other into a seat, and indicated to him to get down to eases pronto.

"I'm a collector and dealer in rare books. My business is an exclusive one and carried out by private transactions with other individual collectors, though on occasions, when I happen to acquire an appropriate rarity, I do deal with museums and famous libraries. However, as I say, it's mostly through private channels."

Edwin Gale coughed, hesitated, crossed a perfectly creased trouser-leg over the other, and came to the point. "Recently a most wonderful rarity came into my possession: *The Secret Memoirs of Caesar Borgia*, written during his imprisonment in Spain, 1496-1506. A priceless relic, as you may well imagine."

"I can imagine somebody borrowing it and forgetting to return it, if that's what you mean," Mr. Brett said.

The other nodded grimly. "You have grasped the

situation at once."

"That's what I'm paid for," Mr. Brett said briskly. "Any idea who the absent-minded—er—booklover is in this case?"

Mr. Gale hesitated a moment before he said slowly: "I am pretty certain, though I can't be positive."

"What's his name and why d'you suspect him?"

"His name's Spencer. Vere Spencer. A young man, rather likeable, as a matter of fact. A woman friend of mine brought him to a little party I gave last week at my flat. In the course of a conversation we had together, he told me he was interested in my line of business, suggested he sometimes acted as a sort of agent for collectors, and if I ever had anything which he might be able to do something about, would I let him know and all that sort of thing. I mentioned this volume of *Borgia Memoirs.* He seemed very keen, begged me to let him see the book. So I took him along to my study. He was vastly intrigued by the relic, said he'd get in touch with one or two people he knew quietly, and he might be able to effect a deal to our mutual satisfaction. I didn't take him very seriously, but told him if an attractive offer came via him, well, I would, of course, consider it. Afterwards, when my guests had gone, the book was nowhere to be seen."

"Did you lock it away after you'd shown it to Spencer?"

"I'm afraid I omitted to. I returned it to the drawer in my desk and forgot to turn the key."

"That was careless of you, wasn't it, Mr. Gale? I

presume it was possible for Spencer to slip into the study during the party and pinch the book?"

"That is what I suspected had happened," he admitted.

"When did this occur?"

"A week ago."

"Why so long calling me in?"

"Well, it was rather embarrassing. I couldn't be *certain* Spencer had taken the *Memoirs*. It might have been one of my other guests."

"Or a servant?"

He shook his head, "My manservant has been with me too long, he has my complete confidence. While the daily help is, of course, ruled out."

"Who else of the guests might have been implicated?"

Again that slight hesitation. Then: "I'm afraid there is no one. They were all personal friends of mine, and I cannot believe any of them would have been capable of—of robbing me."

Mr. Brett regarded him for a moment. Then he said through a cloud of cigarette-smoke: "You mentioned that Spencer was brought along by a woman. Did she know much about him?"

"He was an acquaintance of hers, that's all. She'd understood he was something of a collector, and thought I might like to meet him. I—I rang her up the following morning, as a matter of fact, and informed her what had happened. She lunched with me later, and I told her frankly what I suspected. She was very upset, naturally, but was inclined to agree with me that Spencer could be the only one who might have stolen the book."

"Which would seem to imply you haven't considered the possibility that she and Spencer were in this together."

Mr. Gale looked startled for a moment. "Good gracious, no," he exclaimed. "Nothing like that about it, I assure you. It was sheer misfortune that he'd made her acquaintance and she'd introduced him to me. That is," he added hurriedly, "assuming Spencer to be a thief."

"Your story plus a process of elimination makes the assumption a pretty sound idea," said Mr. Brett.

"I suppose you're right."

"So you'd like me to recover your property. By the way," with a nod in my direction, "my secretary said you wanted to see me urgently. Why the sudden rush, after taking a week to think it over?"

"I have a purchaser for the *Memoirs*," the other said simply. "An American who's going back to New York first thing tomorrow. He leaves London by the boat-train tonight and would have taken the book with him."

"As a matter of interest, or call me nosey, how much would you be soaking him for it?"

Mr. Gale froze slightly. Then he shrugged and said stiffly: "Five thousand pounds."

"No wonder you're steamed up," Mr. Brett smiled thinly. "If I can get the thing back for you by tonight, you'll rake in quite a wad. Five thousand quid, just for an old book," he murmured thoughtfully and. added: "Less my fee."

Edwin Gale said: "This is my suggestion, Mr. Brett. That you satisfy yourself Spencer has the Borgia relic in his possession and offer him five hundred pounds for its return, no questions asked. If you are successful, I suggest two-fifty pounds for your trouble."

Mr. Brett examined the tip of his cigarette. The other watched him silently. After a moment, Mr. Brett looked up and said: "I'll take the case, half of the fee to be paid down now, rest on delivery of the *Memoirs* in time to catch the boat-train tonight."

Gale produced his cheque-book.

"Cash preferred," Mr. Brett smiled at him. He added: "I expect Spencer'll want his that way, too."

The other stared at him his mouth compressed, then without a word took out his notecase. Mr. Brett gave me a nod, "Take care of the gentleman's money," he said.

"If you'll come this way, Mr. Gale," I smiled at him graciously, "I'll give you a receipt." I felt quite indignant on his behalf; Mr. Brett had been quite unnecessarily brusque with him, I thought. But then Mr. Brett never went out of his way to be sweetly polite to his clients. The curious thing was that they seemed to be impressed by his snappiness. Which was probably precisely why he behaved that way. He was lounging back with his feet up on the desk again and calling after me: "Mr. Gale will give you his address and phone number where I can get him any time. Also Spencer's address and number."

"Yes, Mr. Brett," I said.

After Edwin Gale had gone, leaving me with a nice, friendly smile, the speaking-machine on my desk crackled again and I went back to Mr. Brett. "Well," I said, "you must admit I wasn't so far wrong when I told you he'd be the type who talked money." I didn't mention anything about the perfume I'd had given me, he'd only have made some sarcastic remark. "And," I went on, "it looks as if it's going to be one of the easiest two-fifty pounds you ever earned. Just persuade this man Spencer he's got an old book that doesn't belong to him, buy it back with someone else's cash, and the job's done."

"Money for old rope, isn't it?" be said easily. But there was an enigmatic smile at the back of his eyes made me suddenly wonder if he was meaning what he said. He glanced at his wristwatch and murmured: "I'll be paying a call on the character in question presently. You'd better tag along, that exotic personality of yours may help distract him, make it easier for me to winkle out the *Memoirs*." And then he added: "You might dab some of that perfume his nibs gave you behind the ears, they tell me it's wildly intriguing."

I stared at him open-mouthed. How the devil did he know about my nice present? Was he psychic, or had his ear been at the keyhole when Mr. Gale was waiting in my office? But he was only grinning at me in that infuriating way he had, and I realized I was merely looking foolish gaping at him. I closed my mouth so quickly I bit my tongue and went out slamming his door after me. To this day I don't know how he knew about that perfume,

Vere Spencer lived in a small mews flat off Oxford Street. On the corner of the mews Mr. Brett spotted a telephone box. I followed him over to it. I heard him dialling a number and wait for some time. No reply. He dialled again—presumably to make sure he'd got the right number—still no answer. He came out of the box and gave a nod of satisfaction.

"He's out," he said. He glanced up and down. The mews was deserted, and crossed to the flat, quickly ascending the short iron stairway. "Keep your eyes and ears wide," he snapped and turned his back to me. I watched ready to warn him of the appearance of anyone who might be Spencer, and heard the metallic rattle of those odd-looking keys he sometimes carried. We got to work on the front door. In a few minutes there was a click of the lock and he pushed the door open.

He paused on the threshold and said over his shoulder: "If he shows up while I'm taking a look round give me a quiet call and remember we've mistaken his flat for a friend's, found the door left unlocked—"

"The old routine," I interrupted him.

"The old routine," he said, and went in.

He seemed to be ages, with me every moment expecting someone to appear in the mews, forcing me to tip him off. But only a couple of stray cats slunk into view, plus a whistling errand-boy who drifted in for a quiet smoke and then drifted off again. When Mr.

Brett reappeared and closed the door carefully behind him, my watch told me he'd taken actually only twelve minutes on the job. In which time I knew he'd gone through the flat with a fine toothcomb, at the same time leaving not the faintest sign that anyone had been anywhere near the place. Light-fingered wasn't the word for it when Mr. Brett snooped around. I saw from his face he'd discovered all he needed to discover from his search of Vere Spencer's flat.

We turned into Oxford Street and grabbed a taxi. He leaned back and lit a cigarette. He said: "I'm dropping you at the office, I'm going on to Scotland Yard."

"Scotland Yard?" I stared at him blankly. "But I thought Mr. Gale hired you because he wanted to keep the police out of this?"

He smiled at me bleakly through a puff of cigarette smoke, "I think you've got something there," he said.

I didn't get it all. I said: "Did you find the precious book?"

He nodded, "I found it. '*Secret Memoirs of Caesar Borgia Set Down In His Hand, 1496-1506....*' I only had time for a quick peek at it," he went on, "but it looked pretty interesting."

"Isn't Borgia the chap who dodged around poisoning people on the slightest provocation?"

"He was practically the originator of the cocktail, I'm told," Mr. Brett said absently. I glanced at him sharply. Either some natty little scheme was unwrapping itself behind that faraway look, or he'd merely been reminded he could do with a drink, and was deciding on a dive to pop into on his way to Scotland Yard.

When he dropped me at the office, he said: "Be outside the mews in a couple of hours' time. That little heart-to-heart with Spencer is on the schedule just the same, and I'll still want you around to lend your glamour to the conversation." And he leered at me from the taxi,

"Yes, Mr. Brett." I said with my nose in the air, and he pushed off.

I was there waiting for him on the corner of the mews when he got out of his taxi and loomed up out of the dusk.

"Spencer's at home now," I was able to tell him. "There's a light in the window and I caught a glimpse of a man in the flat; I took it to be him."

He grinned at me over the glowing tip of his cigarette. "So you do sometimes have an eye for business other than how your frock's showing off your figure," he said. Which coming from him was quite a compliment.

The man I'd seen in the flat opened the door to us. He was wearing a dressing gown over his evening shirt, and a long cigarette-holder stuck from the corner of a thin mouth. He stared at us and his expression didn't exactly exhibit wild delight at our presence.

"Who are you, and what d'you want?"

Mr. Brett told him who we were, "A certain Mr. Gale is wondering if you've finished with the book you borrowed, because he'd like it back." He added: "If you were polite, you'd invite us in."

The other hesitated, then glanced down at Mr. Brett's foot, which was strategically placed to prevent the door being closed. He shrugged and stood aside. It was a comfortably furnished flat, and its owner obviously wasn't doing so badly out of the book-borrowing business. He was saying:

"I don't quite get what you mean about my having anything belonging to Mr. Gale, perhaps you can be a bit more explicit?"

Mr. Brett smiled agreeably, "A week ago you pinched a volume from him entitled '*The Secret Memoirs of Caesar Borgia*'. It's a valuable relic and I'm hired to get it back. It's as simple as that, really."

Spencer smiled with excessive charm. "It would be—if I knew what in hell you were talking about."

Mr. Brett stifled a tiny yawn of boredom and said, his tone slightly weary: "You'll find it in that bureau in the corner. Second left-hand drawer. Save a lot of argument if you came across."

Spencer nearly swallowed his cigarette-holder in his astonishment. Involuntarily he betrayed his knowledge of the whereabouts of the stolen property by backing in the direction of the bureau as if to ward off any movement towards it. He pulled himself up with a jerk as he realized the significance of his action, and stared at us with a baffled expression.

Mr. Brett regarded him with a saturnine smile. He murmured:

"Maybe I should mention that in return for the

Memoirs I'm to hand you five hundred quid cash, no questions asked."

The other's aggressive attitude relaxed. He smiled—it made me think of a wolf about to walk into a flock of lambs—and drew calmly at his cigarette. He eyed the spiral of smoke curling from the holder and said: "Mr. Gale is more than generous. You say you've brought the money with you?"

Mr. Brett gave me a nod, and I took a thick bundle of notes from my handbag. Mr. Brett took them from me and held them up for the other's inspection.

"Well, of course," Spencer said slowly, his gaze rivetted on the wad of money, "that does seem to jar the memory, somewhat."

"You must be kidding," Mr. Brett jeered at him.

Spencer's grin stretched wider, then he turned to the bureau. He pulled open the drawer Mr. Brett had indicated, and drew out what I saw was a book, extremely battered and ancient in appearance. "I fancy this may be what Mr. Gale's thinking of," he said casually over his shoulder. And then suddenly turned with a swift movement and crouched before us, a nasty-looking automatic in his other hand. "Only he's not getting it back—yet," he snarled. "Not until he's a bit *more* generous. To the tune of another five hundred, shall we say?"

He moved towards us, jerking the gun at Mr. Brett. "I'm taking the cash you've so kindly brought on account," he said. "Put it on the table and then get out."

I didn't like the way the tables had been turned on

us at all, and threw Mr. Brett a quick glance to see how he was taking it. To my surprise he pushed the money into his pocket and was lighting a cigarette as casually as you please. As a study in sheer nonchalance it made a pretty enough picture, but to my mind it seemed the wrong moment to pose for it—Spencer's ugly gun looked much too liable to go off—and if Mr. Brett wanted a cigarette surely he could wait till he *and* I were out of range. Now he was saying quietly:

"Nifty-looking device you have there, Spencer. Pity it happens to be unloaded."

I gave a gasp and threw a look at Spencer, saw him press the trigger with a harmless clicking sound as the only result. Then I realized what must have happened and almost laughed out loud. Mr. Brett had taken the precaution of emptying the gun during his snoop-round earlier. He was smiling bleakly himself as he watched Spencer still pulling foolishly at the trigger, then livid-faced throw it down in enraged disgust. Then Mr. Brett didn't look amused any more, he snapped his fingers and motioned the other to pass over the *Borgia Memoirs*. Spencer shrugged his acceptance of defeat and obeyed with a wry grin. Mr. Brett pocketed the precious book.

"I fear," he said blankly, "that in view of your somewhat uncooperative attitude, my client's five hundred pound offer no longer stands." And he handed the crisp bundle back to me. I felt Spencer's gaze follow me it as I slipped it into my handbag again. I thought he started to say something, but he appeared to content himself with giving Mr. Brett a dirty look and let it go at that.

Not that Mr. Brett seemed to mind, for he turned to him with a smile that was almost affable. "Which I think," he said, "just about clinches the—er—transaction. I'm sure my client will be duly pleased with the safe return of his property," patting his pocket.

A curious expression which I took to be a spasm of rage flickered across the other's face and was gone. Then he said in distinctly uncivil tones: "Get the hell out of here, both of you."

Well, there being no reason at all for us to stay, we didn't.

I followed Mr. Brett as he moved quickly out of the mews. He paused at the phone-box on the corner. "What's my client's number?" I told him and waited outside while he telephoned.

He was a few moments talking to Edwin Gale, and when he hung up, I heard him dial again. This time he asked for Inspector Conway's extension, and while I was puzzling over why he could be dragging Scotland Yard into it, I heard him speaking briskly to the Inspector, and caught the name 'Clifford Lang' and the Hotel Magnifique. He rang off, and as he came out of the box I glimpsed the grin on his face. It was all very mysterious, but I didn't ask him a thing until we were in the taxi and he'd told the driver to make it snappy to the Hotel Magnifique.

"And who—just in case I mightn't guess—would be expecting you, at the Magnifique?"

"My client, who is already on his way there, will,

together with the prospective purchaser of this volume, be eagerly awaiting my arrival."

"The American who's catching the boat-train?"

"Exactly. An individual of means named Clifford Lang."

"And where does Inspector Conway come in?" I said.

"Sharp little ears the girl's got," he mocked. Then: "Conway will enter on his cue all right." And left it at that. I was making very little headway trying to figure what it was all in aid of when the taxi drew up outside the Magnifique.

Edwin Gale was waiting by the Reception Office, and his face lit up when he saw us. He came forward quickly; the smoke from his cigar made us think he looked like a steamer puffing on its way.

"I can't thank you enough," he beamed at Mr. Brett as he took the *Borgia Memoirs* from his reverent hands. "Oh," he said suddenly, "the remainder of your fee," He drew out a cheque from his pocket, "All right for you?" he asked, half humorously. "Afraid I haven't the requisite cash on me."

Mr. Brett's smile was not so humorous I thought. But he nodded and took the cheque all right. The other was continuing: "And I really am most grateful to you. You've done me a very great service. Shall we go up to Mr. Lang's suite? He's awaiting this—" he patted the book fondly—"with keen anticipation, If you'd care to join us in a little drink—?"

"We're right with you," Mr. Brett said with alacrity.

In the lift Mr. Gale burbled away about his old book, pointing out to me its travel-stained appearance and yellow faded pages.

"Yes, it's had a chequered history. Drifted round Europe over four hundred years. After Borgia's death in—when was it?—in 1507 it fell into the hands of a Castillian nobleman—his name escapes me for the moment. Remained with his family a long time. Then it was stolen, I believe. Found its way to Paris. Later smuggled to this country—and even then its adventures weren't ended." He smiled, flipping the pages and pointed out on extract for me to read. "Interesting bit," he said.

I obliged politely, but, could hardly make out the words, they were so faint.... "'Now I am approaching the third year of durance within these imprisoning walls'...," I read, the rest was all blurred. I picked out some more further down the page.... "'the remembrance of days Caesar Borgia was the holder of the keys to my subjects' freedom and arbiter of their fate still makes most bitter my present circumstance'...."

The lift stopped, saving me from bothering any more over it, and we followed Mr. Gale down the luxuriously carpeted corridor,

"Yes, I guess the volume certainly lives up to your description," Clifford Lang was saying as he concluded his inspection of the book. "It's a rare prize."

We were in the tall American's suite and I was clutching a gin-and-something in an atmosphere of cordial harmony. Mr. Gale was beaming all over the place, the other was quietly friendly and obviously entranced with the idea of paying over a cosy five thousand quid for the mouldy *Memoirs* of Mrs. Borgia's boy. I glanced at Mr. Brett, who was standing somewhat aloof busily tucking himself outside his second large scotch. I seemed to detect a sardonic quirk at the corners of his mouth, which wasn't quite in key with the pervading geniality, but maybe it was merely a fly in his drink.

Edwin Gale was saying to the American: "It is an interesting relic, and I must say I feel a wrench letting it go." His expression was quite rueful. I smiled at him sympathetically.

"Perhaps Mr. Lang's cash compensation will ease the pangs of parting," I offered brightly.

Both he and the other laughed and Mr. Gale burbled; "It'll be something to console me. All the same—" and he gave the book an affectionate farewell pat—"it's going a long, long way, away."

Mr. Brett moved in and said over the rim of his glass:

"If you're finding it too heartbreaking, we might arrange for the journey to be cancelled."

There was an edge to his voice, which made me look at him quickly. After a moment's silence, I heard Edwin Gale say: "I don't get you," And suddenly the atmosphere of the room changed. There was a chill menace in the air.

Mr. Brett carefully gulped off the rest of his drink then said: "Maybe my friend Inspector Conway will make my meaning clearer."

The other's jaw dropped, then his eyes narrowed to slits of fury.

"Police? What the hell are you driving at?"

Mr. Brett spoke casually to Clifford Lang. "Go ahead, call the Inspector in."

"You bet," said the American with enthusiasm and sprang to the door connecting with the bedroom, throwing it wide. Inspector Conway stood framed in the doorway formidably backed up by another plain-clothes man behind him. "Come right on in, Inspector," went on Lang unnecessarily, both men were already bearing down on a stupefied Mr. Gale, "I guess you've heard all you need."

Edwin Gale, on being formally charged with attempting to obtain money by false pretences, put up quite a good show of bluster and protest at first. In the end, however, he went quietly.

"Yes," mused Mr. Brett through a cloud of cigarette-smoke some time later, "he did a pretty convincing job. All that act about the book being pinched, and hiring me to recover it from Spencer—"

"Spencer was in it, too?" I said.

Mr. Brett nodded, "Up to the neck. He'll have been picked up by now."

"All with the idea of hoodwinking the American?"

"He was afraid if Lang had it in his possession too long he'd discover it was a phoney. Fixing me to bring it along like that just before he sailed gave him little chance to examine it thoroughly, and at the same time coloured the whole thing an authentic shade."

"He certainly put plenty of cunning into the job," I said. "And the trouble he must have taken in faking up the so-called *Secret Memoirs*—"

Mr. Brett grinned, thinly, "Imagine ruining the entire artistic effect by one unpardonable error."

"It looked genuine enough to me," I said. "But you tell," smiling at him sweetly.

"He wrote it in *English*."

I closed my eyes in sheer mortification. "Right under my nose," I muttered, "and never saw it. Of course, *Caesar Borgia was Italian*."

Mr. Brett, looking exceedingly smug, went on; "Matter of fact, I had a hunch about Gale from the word go. That's what took me to Scotland Yard, to check his fingerprints I'd got on some of the money he paid me. He had a record all right. I tipped off Conway this evening, he got onto Lang—"

I'd stopped listening. I'd been reminded of something that ought to wipe that infuriating smugness off his face like a sponge. I said: "Pity you let him get away with paying the rest of your fee by cheque, not much use to you now is it, Mr. Brett?"

He merely looked more sardonic than ever.

"I'll try to manage with the five hundred quid which you may recall I was supposed to pay Spencer for the book," he said, patting his pocket, which crackled with the musical sound of crisp banknotes. "Somehow I neglected to return these to my client."

He sighed unconvincingly.

"A trifle forgetful of me, I fear."

THE CASE OF
THE OLD AUNT

I'd noticed the girl who came in with the man, but hadn't paid much attention, except to think idly she was very young and pretty in a pink and white fragile sort of way, and the character she was with looked somehow wrong for her. She was attractive and nice-looking enough at first glance, but a second view didn't register so well. In my job as secretary to Mr. Brett, you learn automatically to look at people a second time, and though you can't always go by faces, of course, there are certain features that can be a warning signal if you know how to interpret them. For instance, there was a hardness in this man's eyes, a rapaciousness about his mouth which told you: watch out.

It was this contrast between the two, plus the fact they sat at a table just across from mine, that drew my attention to them in the first place. But as at the time I was doing all right by a late meal, and not giving a thought to my figure when the waiter brought me some more sautéed potatoes, I hadn't given them more than that passing thought. I'd just left the office after a really tough day, with dear, lovable Mr. Brett (how I wished sometimes he'd throw a cigarette-stub off a tall, tall building and forget to let go) at his most sardonic and infuriating, and was tired and hungry.

I'd just finished my coffee, paid the bill, and was relaxing with a cigarette when the girl across the way suddenly got up from her table. The man said something, seemed to look as if he was trying to pacify her and persuade her to take it easy, but she shook her head, gathered up her things. She was leaving. I was watching the little scene with vague interest, wondering what it was all about. As the girl was about to pass me, she gave me a glance. With a sudden shock I saw the intense unhappiness in her eyes. Frightened too, she was, I got that. And something else. In a fleeting second before she'd passed, that look of misery and fear gave place to a sudden desperate entreaty. As if she'd appealed to me for help. It shook me a little and I stared after her, asking myself if I'd just imagined it, and wondering why she'd picked on me and what could I do about it anyway.

She was gone. The man, who'd hastily settled with a chagrined waiter, left with the untasted fish course on his hands, hurried past my table in the wake of the girl. For a moment I set there, tapping the ash off my cigarette. It was none of my business, poking my nose into it would get me precisely nowhere at all. Think me a soft-hearted dope if you like, but I couldn't get over that kid's look. It haunted me. She was badly scared, and unhappy, in need of help. Besides I was curious. Maybe it was that decided me. I got moving.

The man was handing the girl into a taxi as I came out onto the street. I caught a phrase of something he said to her: "All right, all *right,* I won't talk about that any more. Just let me see you home—"

As they drove off, the taxi I'd halted slid to the kerb. I said:

"Tail that one in front. If you lose it, I'll break your neck."

I was smiling as I said it, of course. He was a burly figure behind the wheel, and he grinned back at me appraisingly.

"Wouldn't mind a wrestle with you, lady."

I gave him my icy stare, and he chuckled as he slammed the door after me and stepped on it.

The taxi ahead turned off Sloane Street and drew up before one of those small houses with a big rental. My driver pulled up unobtrusively on the other side of the road, and I watched the girl followed by the man pause outside the front door. While she dug in her handbag for the key, the man did all the talking. He still seemed to be trying to calm her. She found her key, said something to him that looked like a curt goodnight, and the door closed on her. The man went back to the taxi. He was just about to get in when he suddenly swung round and stared at the house as if he'd never seen it before. Then he got into the taxi and it moved on.

Well, if I was going to satisfy my curiosity about it all, I'd have to work fast, and within a few moments I had a finger on the doorbell of the small house. I just hoped the girl herself would answer it, because I hadn't the faintest idea who she was, and if a servant or someone answered it'd be a bit tricky for me. However, my luck was in. It was she who stood framed in the doorway. I saw how slim and young she was, and tired-looking. She recognized me first look and gasped, her hand to her throat.

I smiled at her. "I hope it's not little Miss Butt-in," I said. "Or that my imagination's been playing me up. But back in that restaurant I had an idea you weren't all that glad to be alive. Had a hunch, too, when you passed me on your way out, you sort of threw me an SOS. I sometimes play my hunches and so—well—here I am."

I realized I was talking exactly like Mr. Brett, and I gave a little smile of amusement to myself at the thought. She was saying in a whisper;

"I don't know what did make me look at you like that—I suppose I was so—so desperate and you seemed to have a—"

"A nice kind face," I finished for her.

"You're very attractive," she said. "But there's something more than that about, you. It's in your eyes, I think, a sort of warm-hearted worldliness made me impulsively appeal to you."

Her voice trailed off. It was all very cosy the things she'd been telling me, and I fairly warmed towards her. It was nice to know, too, I hadn't made a fool of myself. I might have been all wrong about that look she'd given me. Then an idea struck me, and I shot her a sharp glance. Was it all on the level? Was it some sort of plant? But I told myself as I surveyed her, there could be nothing phoney about, the kid. It just wasn't there. Reassured on that score I said:

"Well, what are we going to do about it?"

"About what?"

"About what's on your mind."

"Oh."

There was a moment of silence. I said: "Are you in a jam or aren't you?"

"Yes," she said slowly.

"D'you want me to help you or don't you?"

"I—I—" she broke off. Then: "You shouldn't have come after me. I'm sorry I behaved as I did. There's nothing you can do. Not really."

I eyed her. I wondered if she was trying to tell me politely she'd decided on second thoughts. It was something that didn't—couldn't—concern me. I shrugged. "Right, my dear. If you're sure. Only it could be that you were right to pick on me. Maybe I'm your Fairy Godmother who could put everything tidy for you."

She looked at me and said hesitantly: "Who are you?"

I had nothing to lose by telling her. When I added with elaborate casualness I was secretary to a private detective, she stared at me with sudden interest. "A private detective?"

"Martin Brett," I nodded. "You may have heard of him."

She shook her head and I decided maybe they aren't the type who would have heard of Mr. Brett. After a little pause she said slowly: "Would you care to come in for a minute?"

This was a bit of a change from her a minute ago wanting me on my way, and I said, "Why, think my magic wand might come in handy after all?"

"I think you've given me an idea," she said and there seemed to be something ticking over at the back of her mind. A little while later found me in a quiet, nicely-furnished sitting-room with coffee and a cigarette listening to her story. The coffee was delicious, and if the story wasn't the most original and intriguing I'd ever listened to, I managed to fasten my interest on it. It went like this:

The kid's name was Diana Marsh, parents abroad, she was in the house alone except for an ancient house-keeper. Engaged to be married to a young man who sounded like a prize mug, but she was crazy over him, so that was that. The character lived with a rich old aunt, his only relative, who supplied him with allow-ance; and on her death quite a slab of dough would come his way. Miss Christine Rowland her name is, and the old girl dotes on him. Only fly in the cream: the boy was a gambling fool, and one thing that sends Aunt Christine off the handle is gambling. The boy had been involved in trouble at his university, resulting in a premature departure from that seat of learning and a warning from Auntie he'd got to lose his taste for games of chance pronto, or he could say *adios* to his allowance, and she'll will her dough to cats' home, or words to that effect.

Well, I didn't have to be exactly psychic to guess what was coming next. The boy continues gambling, gets mixed up with bunch of playmates, and pretty soon is in treacle again up to his eyes. The man he owes most to is an egg named Victor Norris. He's the one I'd seen her with in the restaurant. He wants his money, and when the boy says he can't pay, Norris hints maybe the aunt has some jewellery tucked away which she'd never miss.

"Of course, Tony" (boy's name is Tony Rowland) "was horrified and refused," the girl said.

I said: "So Norris says all right, only pay up by a certain date, or I go to your aunt?"

She gave me a little look as if surprised I could guess so much, then nodded. "Tony is desperate. There's no one to whom he can turn."

"How much does he owe?"

"Twelve thousand pounds."

I whistled. Money like that doesn't grow on trees. Young Tony was certainly in a spot all right. I said, still sounding like Mr. Brett I think to myself, "And where exactly do you figure in this?"

"I got in touch with Norris. I thought I might persuade him to give Tony time, a chance in which to pay. Not to ruin him."

"And—?"

"You saw us together tonight. His answer was I should persuade Tony to get the jewellery. He argued they would be Tony's one day anyway, why shouldn't he have them now, when they'd be the most use to him." Suddenly she broke down and cried like a baby. "Oh, it's horrible," she moaned, "I know Tony's weak and foolish—but if once we were married, he would have settled down. I'd have made him pull himself together—but if his aunt throws him out, it'll be the finish of him. We shan't be able to marry and he'll go from bad to worse—"

I watched her crumpling her handkerchief into a ball. "I thought I'd given you an idea?" I reminded her.

She looked up at me and blew her nose. "It was—it was just clutching at a straw," she shook her head. "I thought perhaps your Mr. Brett might—might be able to do something. But I don't see how he could."

I frowned a little. Frankly, I didn't see what Mr. Brett could do, either. It wasn't the sort of case he'd take on, and he certainly wouldn't do it just to please me. On the other hand—I gave a little cough, and said: "Er— well, I could ask Mr. Brett. Only thing is the question of his fee—he works on a strictly business basis—" I mumbled on feeling somewhat hot under the collar as I tried to apologize for Mr. Brett's cold cash calculating-machine that served in place of his heart.

She said at once: "I've a little money. Of course, I'd expect to pay his fee—if he could save Tony."

"If he can't, no one else can," I said with conviction. "And he'll tell you frankly yes or no. If it's yes, your worry is over."

Her face brightened and I went on: "Be at the office eleven tomorrow morning. I'll take you into him," and I gave her the address.

* * * * * * *

I told Mr. Brett all about it after I had taken in his mail the next morning. He'd come in rather earlier than usual as a matter of fact, interrupting my routine reading of the newspapers, and was looking more saturnine than ever. I decided privately getting up early didn't suit him. He didn't say a word while I told him how I'd first of all noticed Diana Marsh and the man at the restaurant, then followed their taxi and had learned the girl's story. He just balanced himself in his chair with his feet inevitably on the desk and stared through the cigarette smoke at the ceiling. Even when I ended up with: "Well I hope you're pleased I've booked a client for you—I think she's got enough for your fee anyway," he didn't look in the least bit interested.

He murmured, still staring at the ceiling: "You say you fixed her to see me at eleven?"

"Yes, Mr. Brett."

He was silent for a moment. Then: "Might as well take a view of your little innocent, I suppose."

Something in his voice made me ask slowly: "You think she was merely leading me up the garden?" And I recalled the sudden thought I'd had last night that maybe Diana Marsh wasn't all she made out to be.

"I have a suspicious nature," he said through a puff of cigarette smoke, "and believe everyone's a liar until I find out the truth." He yawned elaborately. "But obviously, my Gorgeous Girl Gumshoe," he went on sardonically, "you haven't read this morning's papers." And while I was burning up with fury at his gratuitously familiar tone, he swung his feet to the floor and pushed a newspaper across to me. "Front page," he said. "Stop Press."

I looked where he indicated and could hardly credit my peepers. But there it was all right, in black and white:

ELDERLY SPINSTER FOUND DEAD

In the early hours of the morning Miss Christine Sims was found dead at her house in Park Square, W.1., in suspicious circumstances. Woman's nephew, Anthony Rowland, discovered the body and at once notified the police. It is understood Scotland Yard are making enquiries with regard to the tragedy."

I gaped at Mr. Brett over the newspaper and he leered back at me.

"What price your innocent friend now?"

"But Mr. Brett," I protested, "what makes you think she had anything to do with this?"

He shrugged. "'Maybe no, maybe yes. Who can tell? She'd have lost a potential rich hubby if Auntie had kicked Rowland out, don't forget. Now she's got him plus legacy safely hooked and Norris can go fly a kite."

I shook my head slowly. "She was desperately scared of Norris when I saw her, of that I'm positive. And why should she fix herself up in murder *after* she'd discovered who I was and agreed to come and see you?" I went on: "Besides, she just isn't the sort who could do anything like that."

"Maybe she's merely an accessory before or after the fact," he conceded. Which was generous of him, I thought, in a repulsive kind of way.

I said thoughtfully: "My bet would be the boy could have done it—"

The phone jangled into life. Mr. Brett grinned at it. "My bet would be it's the Marsh piece cancelling her appointment," he murmured.

He was right about it being her, but she didn't want to cancel her appointment exactly. She wanted to see Mr. Brett more urgently than ever. When was the earliest he could manage it?

"I've seen the papers," I told her gently. "What a terrible shock for you—"

"Worse still has happened," she cut in, her voice hitting a hysterical note. "Tony—*they suspect Tony*—"

She babbled on about how the police had questioned him (it appeared it was he who'd found his aunt dead), warned him not to leave the house, and he was left in dread suspense, convinced his arrest on charge of murdering his aunt was imminent. "He's innocent— he's innocent, Mr. Brett can prove it, I know—I must see him as soon as possible—"

"If you'll hold on, I'll ask Mr. Brett If he can be available earlier," I said. I covered the receiver and raised a questioning eyebrow at Mr. Brett.

"I'll see her when she gets here," he said succinctly and put his feet on the desk again. I gave the girl his message and she said she'd be along in twenty minutes.

When I'd hung up, Mr. Brett said: "Get me Conway."
As I got through to Scotland Yard he added: "Better
listen in, take notes."

Detective-Inspector Conway came on the line and I
went into my office to listen to him and Mr. Brett on
my extension. The C.I.D. man was saying with his typically heavy-handed humour: "Who's your client in this
case, Brett? Don't tell me it's the woman's nephew."

"I don't tell you," said Mr. Brett.

"No, I've never known you to be on the wrong horse
yet."

"There's always a first time," Mr. Brett said agreeably. Then; "So you don't fancy Rowland's chances?"

"Frankly, not much."

"Since you mention being frank, what d'you know?"

"He found his aunt in her bedroom at one-thirty
this morning with her head dented. Been awakened
by some noise he said. Signs of a struggle and her
jewellery—family heirloom stuff—gone. He calls the
doctor, which is a waste of time, she was dead—and
us. That's *his* story. Well, it's all right, of course—only
he's the sole heir and the old girl didn't do herself in.
Admittedly, it seemed possible it could have been an
outside job—fact of the jewellery being pinched, for
one thing—"

"I was thinking the theft doesn't fit in with the theory
Rowland bumped off Auntie to get his hooks on the
legacy a bit quicker."

"No, but the boy's no fool. Our idea is he shifted
the stuff deliberately to throw suspicion on someone

outside."

"You sound pretty definite about his guilt."

"We've had a tip-off which makes it look even more definite. It appears Rowland, who's a bit of a playboy type, was up to the neck in gambling debts and if his aunt had found out she'd have disowned him."

"Who tipped you that information?"

"Some woman phoned, wouldn't give her name. It's my belief she knew something, all right."

"On the other hand," Mr. Brett said after a moment, "was there any evidence to show it *could* have been an outside job?"

"Thought you said Rowland isn't your client?" Conway chuckled meaningfully.

"I'm working for his girlfriend," Mr. Brett said, adding: "I think."

"Well, bedroom's on first floor overlooking a small garden back of the house. Balcony outside which could be fairly easily reached from the garden, admittedly. Rowland stated the window opening onto the balcony was in fact ajar when he entered the bedroom. But the aunt may have left it open, or he may have opened it to give the impression someone had entered and exited that way. But there were no signs the window'd been forced, no traces whatsoever on the balcony—or in the garden anyone had come or gone that way." And the Detective-Inspector bit out this point with emphasis.

"Doesn't look as if Rowland's as smart as you make him out," Mr. Brett said slowly, "You'd think he'd have thought of that, wouldn't you?" And I caught a slightly sardonic edge to his tone.

"You know the saying: the criminal always makes a mistake," Conway chortled back. "Wouldn't be criminals if they didn't."

"What would they be—detective-inspectors?"

But I think Conway missed the finer subtlety of that remark. He only just guffawed. Followed a little heavy-handed badinage from the C.I.D. man, and Mr. Brett rang off.

A few minutes later Diana Marsh turned up. She looked pretty grim and I felt genuinely sorry for her, knowing as I did that her boyfriend seemed to be for it. Mr. Brett glowered morosely out of the window as if he was expecting it to pour with rain all the time she talked to him. The only time he showed any interest in what she had to say was when she asked him about his fee. She said Tony knew she was coming to see him, she was to spare no money if it would help tear down the terrible shadow that hung over him. Whether Mr. Brett's sudden interest lay in the prospect of handling a nice slice of dough, or whether he was commenting privately (as I was) on young Rowland's readiness with his dead aunt's money before it had actually been made over to him, I wouldn't know. Not that the poor young devil could be blamed for acting like that anyway.

Diana Marsh added nothing of importance to Mr. Brett's knowledge of the set-up already learned from Inspector Conway and from me. And he didn't appear to be in the least bit stirred by her pathetic helplessness, her desperate appeal for help. He ended the interview with typical brusqueness.

"I'll handle the case. It'll make a change to take on a job with all the cards stacked against me—my secretary will fix the fee."

After she'd gone, I went back into his office. He was on his way out. He glanced at his wristwatch and grinned at me. "Just popping out for a quick one," he said. At the door he turned. "By the way, you know Victor Norris's address?"

I nodded. I'd made a note of it when the Marsh girl mentioned it earlier. It was a flat in a block off Tottenham Court Road. Mr. Brett said; "Meet me outside the place in an hour's time."

I stared at him a little puzzled. "What d'you think he'll know?" I said. And added: "If he's at home to tell you."

"He'll probably be out," he murmured and I gave him a sharp look. But his expression was enigmatic. The door closed after him and I stood frowning to myself as his footsteps faded along the passage.

An hour later found me waiting by the entrance to the flats. It was a large barn of a building, and as I paced up and down I caught glimpses of an over-decorated vestibule beyond the swing-doors. Mr. Brett arrived in a few minutes and we went up in the self-operated lift.

"I suppose you think I've spent the entire time since I left you propping up a bar?" he jeered at me.

I looked at him wide-eyed. "Frankly, Mr. Brett," I said, "I hadn't given it a thought. I expect I was too busy. You know," I added sweetly, "office routine still operates even when you're out."

But the sting didn't seem to penetrate. He said, with elaborate casualness: "In case you're interested, I spent a while taking a look at a house in Park Square."

"See Tony Rowland?" I asked him.

He shook his head. "Just the outside of the house," he said and contemplated the tip of his cigarette. The lift stopped at the fourth floor and we got out. As Mr. Brett pressed a long finger against the bell push of Victor Norris's flat, I said quickly: "Suppose he *is* in?"

"That's why I brought you along," he said blandly. "To dazzle him with your glamorous charms, maybe put him off his guard at the crucial moment."

He grinned at me sardonically but I wasn't amused. I eyed him coldly. I resented his bright idea he'd been getting lately I could be dragged round as a sort of decoy duck. Then we heard someone on the other side of the door and he hissed mockingly in my ear: "Don't forget to waggle your eyelashes at him, Gorgeous—I'm told it knocks 'em flat."

But it was a woman who faced us. A tough-looking redhead obviously didn't care for our appearances one little bit. But she risked her displeasure to ogle Mr. Brett coyly.

"What d'you want—tall, dark, and not unhandsome?" she said from the side of her mouth. Mr. Brett blew a cloud of cigarette smoke in her dial in a most ungentlemanly way.

"It definitely wouldn't be you," he muttered, and while the redhead was getting the smoke out of her eyes he'd pushed past her. I stuck close to him as I could without actually getting under his coat. The tiny hall led to a lounge and Victor Norris faced us scowling all over his face at us.

"What's-the-big-idea-who-the-hell-are-you-get-out," he rasped all in one vehement mouthful.

Unabashed Mr. Brett said: "The big idea is I'm a private detective hired by a certain Miss Diana Marsh. And believe me I'll get out just as soon as you've answered one or two questions." He went on with smooth affability: "The name's Brett, you're Victor Norris, correct me if I'm wrong."

Norris was looking past us, and I turned to see the redhead behind us. He said to her: "All right, I'll see you later. Meet me at the club for lunch."

The woman stood there for a moment, then went, and a moment later the front door slammed.

"A friend of mine," Norris said.

"Don't apologize," Mr. Brett murmured, and the other shot a nasty look at him. He turned to stare at me as if he was wondering if he'd seen me before. I let him wonder and he said to Mr. Brett:

"What's Diana Marsh got to do with me?"

"Not a thing—beyond the fact you advised her if young Rowland didn't pinch his aunt's jewellery it'd be too bad for him."

"That's a damned lie."

Mr. Brett shrugged. "I see it embarrassed you, so let's talk about something else. About, for instance, your—er—friend just departed." He paused to tap the ash off his cigarette. "This morning someone phoned Scotland Yard, tipped them off about Rowland being neck-deep in debt, and that he would benefit more than somewhat by his aunt's will. You get the implication?"

Norris looked at him coldly. "I thought you would," Mr. Brett purred. "The caller was a woman, and the cops checked the call-box she used. Naturally she'd gone, but they found a strand of hair caught in the receiver. It was red hair." And he drew slowly at his cigarette.

I saw a shadow of uneasiness flicker across the other's face as I wondered how Mr. Brett had got hold of this tasty morsel of information. Norris said: "My friend's not the only red-haired woman who's ever used a phone-box—if that's what you're getting at."

Mr. Brett permitted a mirthless smile to quirk the corners of his mouth. "I'm glad you're keeping in step with me. But maybe you'll agree it's too coincidental to be true that the mysterious redhead also knew something not exactly common knowledge concerning Rowland? Knowledge, which, for example, you could have imparted to her."

The silence was pretty tense.

Then Norris drew a deep breath. "You're smart at putting two and two together, aren't you?"

"I went to school," Mr. Brett said.

"Okay," the other said. "I did get her to make that anonymous call. When I read about Rowland's aunt this morning, I felt in my bones he'd done it. Thought the police might like to know a few facts about that nasty piece of work, her nephew. The twister owed me twelve thousand quid and told me I could whistle for it." He added hurriedly; "That yarn that I tried to get him to knock off the woman's bric-a-brac is laughable, of course."

It didn't seem to be amusing Mr. Brett. He said quietly: "If I were to mention I know the robbery was in fact an outside job, that Rowland is in the clear, what would you say?"

The other laughed, not a very nice laugh. "I'd say where's the proof?"

"On the dining room window which faces the street. Fresh marks indicating the catch was forced. The intruder got in, and no doubt out, that way. He made a cunning job of it. Leaving the bedroom window open with no scratch or footmarks on the balcony or in the garden would, he calculated, set the police figuring Rowland had made a futile attempt to shift suspicion onto someone breaking in from the garden. He figured no one would tumble to the marks on the dining room window through which *he* had popped." He smiled thinly. "He was right," he went on easily, "almost. No one did tumble to it—except me."

Norris shifted his neck in his collar. "Pretty neat of you," he said coolly. "Though it seems to me Rowland still might be an accomplice of this other whoever-he-is. He could have been working on the inside."

"If he was," Mr. Brett purred, "Why didn't he make it easier for his pal to get in? Instead of leaving him to fiddle with the window-latch and risk being spotted by a passing cop?"

"Got it all parcelled-up haven't you?" the other sneered. Then he said with a brisk heartiness: "Well, thanks very much for showing me the way a sleuth's mind works. It's been very interesting, but you'll have to excuse me now."

Mr. Brett's only move was to stub out his cigarette. I watched him crush it to shreds in the ashtray and waited for what was coming next, my mind a little bit foggy, hoping we'd get out without any ugly scene. Victor Norris was saying; "Unless there's anything more you'd like to know from me?" And added: "Afraid I can't confess to being your mystery man, if that's what you're hoping." He laughed, again not very nicely. "I'm not the type who can scheme things out like that. Besides, I've got one of those cast-iron alibis you sometimes hear about."

Mr. Brett glanced at him; "Is that so?"

The other nodded emphatically. "I was right here in this dinky little flat at half-past one this morning, entertaining friends."

"The party including our red-haired acquaintance?" Mr. Brett asked slowly.

Norris hesitated. Then: "Yes, she was here, and a couple from a flat in this building. So there you are."

"Thanks for the information." And Mr. Brett turned to me with a nod indicating we were moving. At the door he paused, lit a fresh cigarette, and observed: "Hope you won't be late for your luncheon engagement."

In the lift I said: "What now, Mr. Brett? Or am I too young to know?"

He grinned at me sardonically. "It'll be a fairly old-fashioned routine," he said. "While Victor Norris is hurriedly packing, we call the police, who'll just hang around and pick him up when he comes out. The betting is Auntie's—er—bric-a-brac will be wrapped up in his shirts and socks."

Mr. Brett was right, of course. The police collared Norris, suitcase and all, about half-an-hour later as he was stepping into a taxi. He fought like a demon, but it got him nowhere at all, at least nowhere he wanted to go to. Mr. Brett was wrong about the shirts and socks though. Aunt Christine's jewellery was wrapped in a pair of pale blue pyjamas. But as he said later when I chided him gently about it:

"It wasn't such a whale of a mistake as he made when he yapped about being at his flat at one-thirty yesterday morning."

"That was when the murder took place?"

"Exactly. But how did *Norris* know that? It wasn't mentioned in the newspaper report and nobody could have told him. *Yet he'd carefully built up an alibi for the very time the murder was committed.* Which means he must have known too much about it than was good for him."

He chuckled, he was in an almost humanly good humour—he'd got a drink in his hand. I said: "What's so funny?"

"I was thinking about the redhead."

I regarded him quizzically. "Would you care for me to get myself up in a henna shampoo and start leaving bits of my hair all over the office phones?"

He chuckled again. "The red hair caught in the call-box phone came out of *my* head," he said. "With the stuff about the cops checking up where she'd phoned from and the rest. That's what's so funny."

THE CASE OF THE GIRL
IN THE CALL BOX

It was latish, Mr. Brett's office was heavy with the grey-blue haze from the endless succession of cigarettes he'd been smoking, and I was just about to suggest to him that I open the window and let in a gulp of fresh air when the phone on his desk jangled.

"Leave it," Mr. Brett growled as I moved forward to grab the receiver.

I looked at him and shrugged. "Supposing it's someone threatened with having their throat cut?" I murmured brightly as the burr-burr continued.

"Anyone who chooses this time of night for it deserves to get their throat cut," he snapped irritably. "Besides, I've had enough of this racket for one day."

That suited me, too; I was fed up with work and wanted to get home, but after all, business was business, and even if the caller was ringing well after office hours, I didn't like leaving whoever it was unanswered. Still, if Mr. Brett wasn't worrying, why should I work myself up into a nervous breakdown over it?

The phone went on ringing while we pretended not to hear it, and went on clearing up the job we had on hand. It was, in fact, only the routine business concerning a case Mr. Brett had recently taken care of for an insurance company, which ordinarily we'd have carried over to the following day. Only the detailed report being already overdue for delivery to the firm in question, I'd managed to persuade Mr. Brett it really should be finished and done with even if it meant an hour or two late at the office.

The phone continued to jangle. Whoever it was thought they needed Mr. Brett's help seemed to be in a pretty persistent frame of mind about it. Mr. Brett scowled at the instrument and finally gave me the nod. As I reached for the darned thing he told me:

"Tell 'em I've taken a trip to Tanganyika."

"Mr. Martin Brett's office," I said, trying to convey by my tone that it was through some supreme miracle the phone *was* being answered. A girl's voice came over the wire, and she sounded in a panic all right.

"I prayed someone might be there," she said, all choked and breathless. "II know it's late, but if Mr. Brett—"

"I'm afraid Mr. Brett—" I began with the automatically weary note well laid on. But she cut in.

"Oh, I'm sure he's gone—but if you could please tell me where I could find him—" Oh, yes, she was persistent, but there was such entreaty behind her words, I somehow felt it wasn't a pet Peke she'd lost in the park, or her paste-earring she'd dropped on a bus.

"If you could give me some idea," I said glibly, "perhaps I could help you?"

Out of the corner of my eye I caught Mr. Brett's yawn.

"You're very kind," the girl said, and it struck me it was a nice voice, young but with a certain timbre to it that aroused my sympathy. "But I don't think anyone but Mr. Brett could *really* do anything. You—you see, it's *murder*!"

"Murder!" I said, shooting a look across at Mr. Brett. "Who's murdered who?"

"It's Miss Dalby who's been—" She broke off and went on;

"I don't know who did it. Oh, please, where can I find Mr. Brett? I'm so frightened they'll say it was I—"

"Why should they—?" I began, but she was sobbing brokenly.

"You don't understand! You don't understand—please tell me where Mr. Brett is, I beg you—"

Well, this was all grim stuff to be hearing, and I placed my hand over the receiver and told Mr. Brett: "Some young woman mixed up in a murder or something. Wants you to help her out."

He tapped the end off his cigarette negligently. "I didn't hear you tell her I'd gone to Pago-Pago," he said.

The voice over the wire was burbling in my ear. I couldn't catch all of it, but I got something about: "I'll kill myself— It's driving me out of my mi—I'll commit suicide—

I said to him; "She sounds the young hysterical type. Maybe if you spoke to her—"

"The young hysterical type is my favourite kind of

client," he jeered. Then: "where's she talking from?" he said but without the slightest interest.

I asked the girl.

"From a phone-box by Regent's Park. I daren't—I *can't* go back to the flat."

"Hold on," I said, "I'll see if I can find out where Mr. Brett may be."

"She's at a call-box," I said to Mr. Brett, muffling the phone again. "Regent's Park way. She really sounds in a jam."

He surveyed me through a cloud of cigarette smoke. "What d'you think I should do about it, Gorgeous?"

I flashed back icily: "Shall I ask her how much money she's got to spend?"

He stared at me, his eyes widening. "Anyone'd think I'm interested only in getting my fee out of people," he purred.

I didn't make the obvious comeback, it wasn't worth it, besides I was frankly perturbed about the girl at the other end of the phone. I had the idea she was pretty desperate, and it mightn't be so good for the Martin Brett office if we brushed her off and left her to go jump off a very high building or take an overdose of sleeping tablets. I said into the phone:

"I'm just checking up where Mr. Brett's gone to—it's possible he's coming back presently, as it happens—" Mr. Brett gave me a sour grimace, but I didn't let it bother me—"meantime, if you could tell me a bit more about yourself?"

"Oh, thank you. Thank you so much—" she said

fervently. "My name's Mary Harcourt. I'm secretary-companion—or *was*—to Miss Dalby—"

While she was talking, I said across to Mr. Brett again:

"She's secretary-companion to one of those well-off spinsters. Might be something in it for you after all." And smiled at him sweetly.

He tried not to look suddenly interested but didn't succeed too well. "Maybe I *could* have just got back from wherever I've been," he suggested, grinning sardonically,

I said to the girl quickly:

"Hold on a moment, I think I hear Mr. Brett coming in—"

"How wonderful—!"

"Yes," I went on after an appropriate pause. "It *is* him. Just wait please, while I have a word with him," I put down the receiver and looked at Mr. Brett questioningly.

"Ask her where we can pick her up," he muttered in a low voice. "Tell her to wait there. I'll be along as soon as possible."

"Yes, Mr. Brett."

The girl said she'd wait outside the call-box, giving me exact directions where it was, and I told her to stick around until we showed up. She was still babbling her gratitude at me when I hung up.

In the taxi on the way Mr. Brett observed with a certain moroseness: "Matter of fact, if it's the well-off spinster who's been bumped off, she *won't* be handing out the fee."

"Maybe she'll have left it all to the secretary, so you'll be able to send her the bill," I said, trying to cheer him up.

His long face limned in the glow of his cigarette was bitter as he turned to me. "Rich spinsters *always* leave their cash to cats' homes," he said emphatically, "particularly cats' hones already bulging with fat legacies, Seldom does the poor secretary-companion get a sniff at a brass farthing. It's a way rich spinsters have, and something should be done about it."

"Such as leaving their money to a fund for retired private detectives?" I said,

He said: "I had already thought of that."

Mr. Brett left me to pay off the taxi as we pulled up alongside the call-box while he went over to the girl who stood waiting expectantly in the pool of light from a street-lamp. As I joined him—taking a mental note of the fare to take out of the petty cash—I heard her telling him:

"She's dead, Mr. Brett." She spoke in hurried gasps, blurting out the words as if they'd been bottled up inside her. "I went out just now to post the letters—I do every evening, you see—and when I came back I found her—" She broke off and her voice hit a high note of near-hysteria. "I didn't do it—I didn't—"

He cut in: "Try and relax. Just tell me what happened and don't rush it. Don't rush any of it."

She gave him a grateful look.

"Yes, Mr. Brett. Oh, thank heavens I managed to find

you. I'd read about you in the newspapers and when—this happened—I rushed out. I didn't know what I was doing, then I suddenly thought of you—"

"People often do when they're in trouble," Mr. Brett told her sardonically through a puff of cigarette smoke. Then: "But just you say what you did after yon found your—er—late employer. You took a dive, you were saying?"

"Yes, I lost my head. The way she looked. Oh, it was ghastly." She shuddered violently at the remembered horror. She was a thin-faced girl of about twenty-five, plainly, almost shabbily-dressed, with a crushed air about her that made her seem very pathetic. She continued: "I rushed out of the flat—"

"Without stopping to call a doctor or the cops?" Mr. Brett's tone as he said it was casual. almost conversational. A little too casual, and I gave the girl a quick look. She'd caught that undernote in his voice and she burst out defensively:

"I daren't. You don't understand. They'll say I did it. She was always telling her friends and people—she even told the hall-porter—I hated her, that I'd be glad to see her dead," She broke off again to add pathetically: "Miss Dalby wasn't very nice sometimes. She was cruel—"

Mr. Brett said evenly:

"Supposing we took a look at her?"

"No," she gasped. "I can't—I couldn't face it—"

Mr. Brett regarded the tip of his cigarette. The girl started to cry quietly and I took her arm.

"Take it easy." I said to her. "It'll be all right. If you didn't harm Miss Dalby—and I'm sure you didn't—no one's going to take it out of you."

She dabbed her eyes with a screwed-up handkerchief.

"All right," she said. "I'll go back." She turned to Mr. Brett. "I'm sorry. You must think me an hysterical fool—but—but the shock, I—"

"Couldn't we get going?" he interrupted her, with a touch of impatience.

"It's Parkside Mansions," she said. "Across the road, on the corner of Regent's Crescent."

Parkside Mansions was a small, select-looking block of flats. The glass double doors were open and Mr. Brett paused, glancing into the small softly-lit entrance-hall beyond.

"Porter's on duty," he said to the girl "Did he see you come out?"

She hesitated a moment then: "No, I used the stairs, not the lift. We're only on the second floor."

Mr. Brett nodded and we went in. The porter greeted the girl cheerily, but with an expression of slight surprise. "'Ello, Miss 'Arcourt." He turned to grin at us. He was a somewhat undersized character. Sandy-haired. About forty. I noticed although he was in uniform, he'd no cap, and a cigarette-stub was stuck behind his ear. As we got into the lift, he glanced sympathetically at the girl.

"You seem a bit done-in, Miss, if I may say so." And looked at me as if for confirmation,

I nodded. "Miss Harcourt is a little seedy, but we'll take care of her."

The man pressed the button and we whirred upwards. Again he eyed the girl with that slight air of puzzlement and said: "I didn't notice you go out, Miss 'Arcourt."

She began to stammer something but Mr. Brett butted in with: "You been on duty here all night?"

"I 'ave, as a matter of fact," came the answer, the porter's tone suggesting it wasn't any of Mr. Brett's business anyway. "Sorry you ain't feeling up to the mark." he said to the girl. "'Ope you'll feel better in the mornin'. Second floor."

The lift stopped and we got out.

"Mr. Palmer ain't arrived yet," the porter volunteered through the lift-gates as they slid in front of him, "Good-night," and pressing the button he disappeared from view.

Mr. Brett surveyed the girl.

"Palmer?"

"He's Miss Dalby's solicitor," she explained. Her face lit up with a. wan smile for a moment. "He's an old friend of her family and very kind. I—I'd forgotten he was expected for coffee this evening, he usually looks in once or twice a month. Oh, it'll be horrible for him—"

"You lived with her alone?" Mr. Brett was saying as we moved down the short corridor.

"Yes."

We reached a cream-coloured door and she produced a Yale key from her handbag. We followed her into the small hall. Mr. Brett gazed around him with an abstract air. On the right was a miniature hallstand holding a woman's overcoat, hat, and umbrella. Beyond the hall was a door slightly ajar. The girl nodded to it.

"In—in there," she said shakily.

Mr. Brett glanced at her. "You left the light on," he observed.

The light was in fact burning in the room ahead. She answered half-apologetically. "I must have forgotten it when I rushed out."

She looked a ghastly colour and I took her arm comfortingly. She flashed me a wan grateful little smile.

Mr. Brett said over his shoulder as he strode ahead into the room: "You'd better come in, too."

I followed the girl, who after hesitating pulled herself together and then went in. She hung back as Mr. Brett bent over the bed on which the huddled figure lay. He gave it a cursory survey. "Smothered to death," he murmured half to himself. He stood up and lit a cigarette. He glanced round the bedroom slowly. It was small but nicely furnished. Obviously the late Miss Dalby was cosily off all right.

The girl started to sway a little. "It's dreadful. Dreadful!" she moaned. Mr. Brett glanced at her, then at me and gave me a nod. I crossed quickly and grabbed her arm.

"Sit down," I told her. "And don't look. You don't have to."

She parked herself on the edge of a chair and leaned

back, eyes closed. I stayed near her, watching Mr. Brett. He moved suddenly to the window, at which the curtains fluttered in a draught,

"Window's open," he said.

The Harcourt girl sat up, her eyes widening. "That's funny," she said. "Miss Dalby always closed it in the evening. When she came to bed, which was always very early, she locked her door, too."

"That so?" Mr. Brett said over his shoulder as he leant out of the window. "Leads to the fire escape," He ducked his head back into the room. "Wouldn't have been overwhelmingly tricky for someone to force the catch and pop in and out this way."

"You mean the murderer?" she asked in a low voice.

He turned and regarded her, his face saturnine and sharpened as he rapped back: "No, someone just dropping by to say 'good-night'. He was looking round the room again, speculatively, He said to the girl, his eyes on a small print over by the dressing table, "You say she always locked the door at night?"

"Yes."

"What was she afraid of?"

"Her jewellery. She kept it here."

He said with deceptive casualness. "Any idea where?"

There was a slight pause. Then: "No, Miss Dalby never told me."

Mr. Brett examined the tip of his cigarette with absorbed attention. After a moment he went on: "So she locked herself in. Would she open the door to you?"

"Sometimes. But she didn't like being disturbed. Most nights she used to sit in the armchair reading for a while before going to bed. Sometimes Mr. Palmer would call and see her. He looked after her business in the City, and occasionally he'd come in when he'd been working late and she wanted to know about certain of her business matters. He lives nearby. He'd usually have some coffee with Miss Dalby, I'd take it into them."

"Correct me if I'm being crazy, but I seem to have the impression you weren't exactly devoted to your boss?"

She bit her lip. Then said firmly: "I didn't like her, but she might have been worse. I didn't do *that* to her." She fixed her eyes on the bed for a moment, then closed them with a shiver.

Mr. Brett made no comment. He turned to me: "Entice the porter here, will you? I'd like a word with him, then we'd better call the police,"

"Yes, Mr. Brett," I said, and with a reassuring smile at the girl I beat it.

I was back in a few minutes with the porter who seemed suitably impressed with the horror of the tragedy. "Pore lady, wot a terrible thing to 'ave 'appened," he kept on saying on our way up in the lift. He was apparently deeply affected. "One of the nicest tenants we 'ave—er—'ad—" he carefully corrected himself.

But as he faced Mr. Brett in the bedroom I noticed his pallor and the nervous twitch that had appeared underneath one eye. He was trembling a little also. Might mean nothing, might mean something, I thought.

"Before I call the police," Mr. Brett was telling him, "maybe it'd be an idea to ask you a couple of questions."

"Suits me," said the other promptly. "Only thing is wot right you got? Eh?"

Mr. Brett carefully told him about his rights, and the porter mouthed "Oh" in a subdued gulp and went even paler about the gills.

"Must be an awful shock for you," Mr. Brett said with an oblique glance at the inert shape on the bed. He said it in an almost sympathetic tone, but his eyes were sharp and narrowed.

The man nodded. "'Orrible, it is."

"You the head-porter here?"

"Yessir. Name's Horton, Albert Horton, in case yer wants ter know. Everyone calls me 'Bert' naturally. I got an assistant—'e was on duty this arternoon from midday up till tea-time."

"You've been around since then?"

"'Sright."

"Who've used the lift during that time?"

"Not many." He pondered a moment, pulling at his lower lip. "It was just arter I came on that I took Miss Dillon up to her flat on the third.... Then, 'arf-an-'our later it'd be, I brings Mr. and Mrs. Fulton down from the fourth.... Little arter six 'pip emm' there was Mr. Bell up ter three.... Then—" he paused to scratch the back of his head,

"Anyway, no one *unknown* to you used the lift?"

"No one, sir." Emphatically.

"How about the stairs?" I chimed in helpfully.

Mr. Brett regarded me with a certain sourness, "All right, Dream Girl, I'm taking care of this."

"Sorry, Mr. Brett—"

But he was chatting casually to Horton again. He asked him:

"You took Miss Harcourt down when she went to the post?"

"'Sright."

"And brought her back when she returned?"

The porter looked at the girl with a slight frown creasing his forehead. "Yus," he agreed slowly.

"But you *didn't* bring her down in the lift before she came in with us?"

"No, that's wot puzzled me—when I saw Miss 'Arcourt come in with you. I must have just popped off ter get a cigarette."

Mr. Brett made no comment on that explanation. He merely flicked the ash off his cigarette and murmured thoughtfully: "So you couldn't swear no one slipped up here during that time without your knowing it?"

"I suppose I couldn't swear to that. But they'd 'ave to 'ave been pretty spry. And anyway, 'ow did they get away? I'd 'ave spotted 'em coming down, at least." He shook his head with a knowing air. "No, sir," he said, "I reckon it was someone in the flats done it. O' course, I ain't no detective, but that's my opinion, for what it's worth."

"Which isn't much," Mr. Brett told him succinctly.

Horton said, "Oh" again, and subsided.

Mr. Brett appeared to lose interest in him, and he let his gaze wander round the room while he drew abstractedly at his cigarette. Horton stood uneasily first on one foot then on the other. He glanced at me, then at the Harcourt girl. Then he took the cigarette stub from behind his ear. He was about to light it when he remembered the figure on the bed, and with an air of embarrassment pushed the stub behind his ear again. Mr. Brett, who'd had a cigarette drooping from his mouth all the time, said to him:

"Smoke if you want, Horton, it soothes the nerves."

"Yes, sir. Thanks—I do feel a bit shaky. The shock, I expect."

"I expect so," Mr. Brett nodded—and then suddenly jerked his head up in a tense, listening attitude.

I lent a sharp ear myself and caught the faint humming sound which had attracted Mr. Brett's attention.

It was the lift ascending.

The noise grew louder and the porter exclaimed: "Somebody usin' the lift now."

There was nothing to it, of course. I mean, what's so unusual about people using a lift in a block of flats? But all the same I could feel a momentary tightening of the atmosphere as that humming grew. I found myself remembering something I'd once heard about how the murderer always returns to the scene of his crime. Silly of me, I knew, because even as I gave a slight shiver it occurred to me whoever had bumped off Miss Dalby and wanted a second look would hardly dare to come back quite so openly.

Mr. Brett made me jump to it by suddenly snapping at me: "Cut the dreamy-eyed stuff, Beautiful, and shut the door."

I moved like a flash, and as the lift stopped at the second floor, and I heard the sound of the lift gate sliding open, swiftly closed the bedroom door. Horton and the girl stared at Mr. Brett, who snapped: "Not a squeak from any of you."

"Blimey, wot's the idea—?" began the porter, but Mr. Brett bit out a warning at him.

"Shut up."

The room was eerily silent except for the sound of the porter's somewhat asthmatic breathing, then the electric-bell cut the stillness like a knife. The Harcourt girl gave a gasp.

"It's Mr. Palmer," she exclaimed.

"Stay where you are." Mr. Brett's voice hissed at her.

"But—but he wants to come in," she answered in a low voice. "He—"

"I don't imagine he's ringing just for the hell of it," Mr. Brett muttered. *"Keep quiet."*

The bell rang again. And again.

Followed a long pause. Then suddenly but unmistakably came the scrape of a key in the Yale lock.

"He's got a key," whispered the girl, her voice charged with sudden apprehension. "Mr. Palmer never had a key—"

"If you don't shut up, I'll sock you," Mr. Brett rasped

in a savage undertone.

The front door opened and closed quietly. Footsteps approached and a voice called out, a cheery, plaintive sounding baritone. "Miss Dalby...."

There was a choked gasp from the girl. A pause as if the newcomer was making sure there was no reply, then the bedroom door opened and a thick-set man, slightly bald, stood framed in the doorway. He gazed first at one then another of us in what might be described as some surprise,

"Mr. Palmer!" the girl said but he didn't hear her— his eyes were suddenly fixed on the bed.

"What—what's happened?" he gulped and with a quick movement was at the bedside.

"Miss Dalby's dead," the girl said unnecessarily.

Palmer turned to Mr. Brett questioningly.

"Must be a terrible shock to you," Mr. Brett said, and in answer to the other's query told him who he was and what he was doing there. He remembered to include me in the introduction, too.

"This is ghastly," the solicitor muttered. "Ghastly." He glanced again at the bed. "When—when did it happen?" he asked, taking out a handkerchief and dabbing his face with it.

Mr. Brett said: "Within the last thirty or forty minutes, I'd say."

"Suicide?"

"I think we can dismiss any idea the woman smothered herself. It would be a somewhat unusual way of bumping herself off."

"Miss Dalby *was* slightly eccentric," Palmer offered.

Mr. Brett said gently through a puff of cigarette smoke. "Not all that eccentric."

The other looked at him, frowning. "You mean it's murder?"

Mr. Brett nodded,

"Oughtn't the police to be called in? Whoever did this dreadful thing isn't going to get away with it. I mean," he went on, bringing a touch of apology to his tone, "I'm casting no reflection on your capabilities, Mr. Brent—"

"Brett," Mr. Brett corrected him with a thin smile, "*the* Martin Brett."

"I beg your pardon, Mr. Brett. I was going to say I'm casting no—"

"You needn't give me the speech over again. You want real, live cops on the job. The Scotland Yard business." Mr. Brett threw me a look. "Let's not keep the gentleman waiting. Tell 'em to come running."

I picked up the bedside telephone and dialled the old familiar number. While I was being put through to the extension I wanted, the Harcourt girl suddenly piped up with:

"Mr. Palmer, I never knew you had a key to the flat."

He looked at her with a faint smile. "I didn't, till a moment ago. I found this in the door—after I'd been ringing." He held out the palm of his hand to her and she took the key. "You must have left it there," he said. "Careless of you, my dear."

The girl stared at the key with a puzzled look for a

moment, then started to dig into her handbag, obviously unable to believe she hadn't retained the key. Her search seemed to be fruitless, however, because after a moment she looked up at the solicitor with a rueful expression. "I'm afraid I must have done that," she admitted.

I finished giving the Scotland Yard boy all the necessary details to start them moving fast in our direction and hung up. I looked at Mr. Brett and saw he was eyeing the solicitor with a chilly smile.

"Speaking of being careless," he said to him suddenly. "You've managed to make a mistake or two *yourself* this evening." As Palmer opened his mouth to speak, he went on urbanely as a cobra poised to strike: "Save your breath, you're going to need it one of these early mornings, and I'll tell you what I mean. It goes like this: waiting outside until you saw her"—with a nod at Mary Harcourt—"go to the post, you slipped up here by *the stairs.* No doubt congratulating yourself you'd timed it just when the porter chanced to be off duty for a minute. You got into the flat by that key," indicating the one the girl was holding, "which you'd managed to get hold of somehow, then you knocked on this door in the usual way, and Miss Dalby, unsuspecting, let you in. I can't tell you *why* you preferred her dead—could be you'd been monkeying around with her investments, it's been known to happen— but anyway, when you'd done the job you hopped out through that window. You left it open deliberately to give the idea it was an outside job. Then you turn up here as expected. Any questions?"

"I've never heard such a preposterous rigmarole in all my life," choked Palmer, but his face was beaded with sweat. He took out his handkerchief again. "But as a matter of interest perhaps even a block-headed fool of a so-called detective such as you can offer some evidence for your wild, malicious accusation?"

Mr. Brett grinned at him over his cigarette. "All right, as a matter of interest this prize chump will spill it. One, you forgot to lock the bedroom door behind you. Two, a minute ago you walked in here...obviously knowing it wasn't locked, as it would have been had Miss Dalby been alive."

There was a sudden gasp from the Harcourt girl and the porter as the significance of his words sank in. My eyes were on Palmer, whose mouth was agape, his fingers clutching the handkerchief clenched convulsively.

"If you hadn't known she was dead," Mr. Brett continued remorselessly. "you would never have come barging in, you'd have waited for her to open the door."

The solicitor darted a hunted look round the room, his mouth tightening into a thin line as he saw that the porter had moved forward and stood a tough, formidable figure between him and the door.

Mr. Brett read his thoughts. "I shouldn't try it," he said jeeringly. "You might get hurt."

Suddenly the other seemed to collapse like a deflated balloon. His control went to the winds and he broke out wildly: "I didn't mean to do it. It was an accident.

She struggled—it was an accident—"

The girl gave a horrified cry at this self-admission of guilt.

"Let me go. I'll pay anything. Anything—" Palmer sobbed.

"Save it," Mr. Brett told him coldly.

The other saved it and slumped a trembling, stricken figure into a chair, burying his face in his hands. He stayed that way until the police arrived. As the Scotland Yard inspector—who was a personal friend of Mr. Brett's—was going, Mr. Brett took a Yale key from his pocket.

"By the way," he said with typically elaborate casualness. "You'll be wanting this." To me who was gazing at it with certain curiosity he said: "The Harcourt piece left it lying around when she came into the bedroom."

"And Palmer made out she'd left it in the door," I said.

He nodded. "He had to talk his way out of being in possession of a key himself."

He paused a moment reflectively, then muttered: "Which reminds me. There's one angle of this case I *haven't* straightened yet.

I looked at him quizzically. It seemed to me he'd sewn up every aspect of the entire bag of tricks pretty neatly. I said:

"What would that trifling matter be, Mr. Brett?"

"Trifling matter, hell," said Mr. Brett morosely. "I've got to talk myself out of accepting that darned Scotland Yard cashier's usual mangy fee, and soak him for a *real* chunk of cash for a change."

ABOUT THE AUTHOR
(1908-2006)

by Philip Harbottle

Born in July 1908 in Dudley, Worcestershire as Vivian Ernest Coltman-Allen, **Ernest Dudley** grew up in Cookham, Berkshire, where his father kept a hotel. Stanley Spencer lived next door, and was a friend of the family. Through Spencer's patrons, the hotel became a meeting place for artists and actors. Ivor Novello was a weekend fixture. The comedian and film star Jack Buchanan helped the young Ernest rehearse a song for an amateur concert.

At the age of seventeen Ernest left boarding school and joined a theatre company touring Shakespeare through provincial Ireland, in village halls and cowsheds. From this he graduated to the more upscale Charles Doran Company, and performed in proper theatres, paying its actors the munificent sum of £2 a week. For the rest of life he used and was known by his stage name of Ernest Dudley

Always one with an eye for the ladies, Ernest soon met and teamed up with his late wife, the celebrated actress Jane Grahame.

Jane came from a theatrical family: her stepfather was Ellie Norwood, famous silent film actor who played Sherlock Holmes on stage. Through these family connections, Ernest secured work in the West End, appearing with Charles Laughton and Fay Compton, amongst others. When the original production of Noel Coward's *PRIVATE LIVES* transferred to Broadway, it were he and his wife who were recruited to take over the Laurence Olivier and Gertrude Lawrence roles in the British touring production.

His wife regularly played leading roles in the stage plays of Edgar Wallace, and Ernest would later create for her the character of Miss Frayle, assistant to Dr. Morelle in his radio plays. Other actresses would later take over the role, most notably Sylvia Sims. Amongst the actors who played the good Doctor was Cecil Parker.

In the 1930s and 1940s Dudley worked regularly for the BBC. In July 1942 his famous detective character (modelled on the autocratic film actor, Eric von Stronheim, whom he had met in Paris in the 1930s) 'Dr. Morelle' made his radio debut on *MONDAY NIGHT AT EIGHT*. Dr. Morelle was a big hit with listeners, and engendered a long cycle of novels and short stories, a play and a film, and three series on radio. At around the same time, he launched another very successful radio programme, *THE ARMCHAIR DETECTIVE*, which ran for many years, and Ernest became known as "The BBC Armchair Detective." In this weekly programme he reviewed the best of the current releases of detective novels, dramatising a chapter from each. They included his dramatization of John Russell Fearn's 1947 novel *ONE REMAINED SEATED*, and it was this fact that would cause Fearn's biographer Philip Harbottle to seek Dudley out some fifty years later, to become his friend and agent. Notable amongst his many other radio credits is the fact that he was the first-ever radio jazz critic. In the 1950s he transferred to BBC television with an early audience participation programme, *Judge for Yourself.*

Back in the 1930s Ernest also ran a parallel career as a newspaper journalist, specialising and pioneering in show business gossip, working for a time with Val Guest, with whom he had also earlier worked as a film scriptwriter in the British "quota" studio system. Amongst his many newspaper 'scoops' was how he had collaborated with actor Fred Astaire in a London nightclub on the creation of a new dance step.

All of which only gives the bare bones of an amazing career as, variously, an actor, sports correspondent, jazz critic, playwright, novelist, gossip columnist, screenwriter, and crime reporter. Most amazing is the fact that he became a marathon runner at an age when other people were drawing their pensions and relaxing by the fireside, and competed in several New York Marathons, writing a best-selling book on how he achieved his amazing feats, *RUN FOR YOUR LIFE.*

Apart from some fourteen Dr. Morelle books, Ernest also published during his lifetime a dozen other detective novels, mostly notably *THE HARASSED HERO* (1951) which was subsequently filmed. He also appeared with short stories in leading detective periodicals such as *John Creasey Mystery Magazine* and, in the U.S.A., *Ellery Queen Mystery Magazine*. In the 1960s, and the following decades, he became established as the author of a long series of "animal" books for children, including *RANGI*, the story of a Highland rescue dog, and *RUFUS: THE STORY OF A FOX*. Ernest has also written novelisations of a number of films, along with a range of best-selling non-fiction books on diverse subjects, most notably *CHANCE AND THE FIRE HORSES* (Harvill Press, 1972), bringing to life Victorian London and telling the story of a dog, famous at the time, called Chance, who became attached to the fire brigade, and a favourite of the Prince of Wales.

An expert and enthusiast on the exploits of Sherlock Holmes because of his wife's family connections, Ernest wrote a two-act stage play, *THE RETURN OF SHERLOCK HOLMES*, which was successfully staged and taken on tour in 1993, with Michael Cashman as Holmes.

In 2002 Ernest was introduced to a literary agent, Philip Harbottle, through a mutual friend, Ray Norton. His new agent quickly arranged for a US publisher, Wildside Press, to reprint some of his best detective books, including a number of 'Dr. Morelle' adventures, in print on demand paperback format. Subsequently, the leading English publishers of 'large print' editions,

F. A. Thorpe, began featuring Ernest's detective novels in their Linford Mystery series. As well as his non-series books, all 14 "Dr. Morelle" titles were eventually reprinted, along with new posthumous collections.

Ernest continued researching, writing, and networking with actors and journalists right up to the end of his life. In 2005 he was interviewed on BBC radio by Ned Sherrin, and he continued to submit to the BBC numerous innovative proposals for both television and radio shows, that sadly were not taken up.

He was working on a new Dr. Morelle story based on his original stage play when he suffered a stroke at the beginning of November, 2005. His last completed story was a novelette, 'The Beetle', featuring Edgar Allan Poe's famous detective Auguste Dupin, based on his earlier BBC radio play, *The Flies of Isis*, and written at the suggestion of his literary agent after he had heard a recording of the play. The first of a planned trilogy was accepted for a Canadian anthology of Poe's 'Dupin' stories, to appear alongside pastiche stories by Michael Harrison, John Dickson Carr, and Charles Dickens. Having courageously battled to overcome his first stroke, Ernest was checking the proofs of his story in hospital at the time of his death, following a second attack, on February 1, 2006.

Ernest had been befriended by the noted British journalist and broadcaster Matthew Sweet, whom he had got to know when Matthew was researching for his landmark book on the history of early British cinema, *SHEPPERTON BABYLON* (Faber and Faber, 2005).

Ernest's fascinating anecdotes helped the success of the book, and at the time of his first stroke, Ernest had been set to begin filming with Matthew the second programme of a television adaptation of the book for BBC3. Whilst the Canadian anthology was fated not to appear, 'The Beetle' was included in a new posthumous detective story collection, *DEPARTMENT OF SPOOKS*, published by Borgo Press in 2011. Borgo are currently issuing further titles in his "Dr. Morelle" series, as well as his other private detective characters. including Martin Brett and Nat Craig.

His literary agent was able to complete Ernest's unfinished Dr. Morelle story, 'Locked Room Murder', from the notes Ernest left behind, and other material found in his effects is being assembled for publication on both sides of the Atlantic. Recently published Borgo posthumous titles include *THE RETURN OF SHERLOCK HOLMES* and *NEW CASES FOR DR. MORELLE* (2012).

Ernest Dudley's range of accomplishments was awesome. He would have been immensely proud of the fact that BBC radio have recently broadcast several of the Dr. Morelle episodes starring Cecil Parker, following the discovery of recordings in his effects.

Ernest is survived by a daughter, Susan Dudley-Allen, who works in her own consultancy business in New York City—a remarkable lady in her own right, with a long, distinguished career in the theatre and television. With his agent, she is devotedly overseeing the restoration of an amazing literary career.

www.ingramcontent.com/pod-product-compliance
Lightning Source LLC
Chambersburg PA
CBHW031431250626
47155CB00004B/1696

THE BEARD OF
THE PROPHET

The murder is as impossible as it is horrible. Archeologist Reuben Hayles, following written warnings that his life's in imminent danger, has asked for—and received—police protection at his home. Superintendent Budd has stationed himself outside the door of his room, while Sergeant Leek remains on alert right outside the room's only external window. Neither police officer sees, or hears, any intruder. Yet Hayles is found dead, his face and head battered by some tremendous blow. But apart from his corpse, the room is empty, devoid of any murder weapon—so the blow couldn't have been self-inflicted! A search reveals no hidden panels, so how has the man been killed? A classic crime novel featuring Gerald Verner's most famous detective!

Borgo Press Books by GERALD VERNER

The Beard of the Prophet: A Mr. Budd Classic Crime Tale
The Dragon Princess: A Novel of Adventure

THE BEARD
OF THE
PROPHET

A MR. BUDD
CLASSIC CRIME TALE

GERALD VERNER

THE BORGO PRESS

MMXII

THE BEARD OF THE PROPHET

Copyright © 1939 by Gerald Verner
Copyright © 2011 by Chris Verner

FIRST BORGO PRESS EDITION

Published by Wildside Press LLC

www.wildsidebooks.com

DEDICATION

To Ernest Dudley, with every good wish

CONTENTS

CHAPTER ONE

MR. BUDD HEARS
OF THE PROPHET

That obese and sleepy-eyed detective, Superintendent Robert Budd, always referred afterwards to the queer incidents surrounding the death of old Reuben Hayles as "that hokum business at Liddenhurst." And to a certain extent this description was justified.

The old, neglected manor house and its strange occupant, the storm which raged throughout that terrible night, and the horrible and 'impossible' death of the old man, did not strictly belong to real life at all.

They were, as Mr. Budd remarked disparagingly at the time, 'story book stuff,' and his sense of reality was, in consequence, a little outraged.

The whole thing began on a morning in late August, when he was summoned to the Assistant-Commissioner's room and found Colonel Blair, smooth and dapper as usual, examining the contents of a big folder that lay open on the desk in front of him.

"Sit down, Superintendent." His superior nodded towards a vacant chair. "I've got something rather queer here. You've heard of Reuben Hayles, I suppose?"

"The archaeologist feller?" murmured the big man, and the Assistant-Commissioner inclined his head.

"That's the man," he said. "The newspapers were full of him six months ago. He was supposed to have discovered the tomb of Mohammed. There was great excitement at the time. Professor 'This' said he had, and Professor 'That' said he hadn't. Letters were written to *The Times* praising him and abusing him alternately. He read a paper to the Archaeological Society, proving conclusively that he had found the tomb of the prophet, and another distinguished gentleman read a paper proving equally conclusively that he'd done nothing of the kind. Nobody, apparently, has the least idea which is right."

The fat man blinked sleepily. Certainly he hadn't, and he didn't very much care.

"Well, it appears," continued Colonel Blair, "that this man Hayles has recently been receiving a series of threatening letters. Instead of disregarding them, as the majority of people would, he seems to have taken a serious view. So much so, in fact, that he has asked for police investigation and protection."

"Surely, sir," murmured Mr. Budd, raising his eyebrows in surprise, "it's a matter for the local police to deal with?"

"In the ordinary course, yes," said his superior. "But Hayles is a distant cousin of the Home Secretary, and he has particularly requested that we should look into the matter. Liddenhurst, where Hayles lives, is on the edge of the Metropolitan area, so I'm sending you

down to pacify the old man.

"It's unusual, I know," went on the Assistant-Commissioner, when he saw Mr. Budd's expression, "to detail such a trivial case to any officer of your rank—but the circumstances are exceptional. Personally I don't suppose for one minute that there's anything in these threats. They're the usual sort of twaddle, but there you are." He shrugged his shoulders and flicked open the folder in front of him. "Here are the letters," he said, pushing the cardboard cover across the desk, and Mr. Budd sat forward wearily, and inspected the contents.

They consisted of four sheets of cheap notepaper and the messages, which had been typewritten, were short. The first was dated July 15th, and ran:

"Your sacrilege will bring violent death in its train. Take heed for your time is short."

It was signed: "The Prophet."

And the second, which was dated ten days later read:

"Every passing hour brings your doom nearer. The curse is upon you."

The date of the third was only a week after the second:

"I am coming for you soon. The hand of Mohammed is raised to strike."

There was an interval between this and the last of nearly three weeks, and the threat became more definite:

> "Death will come to you on the night of the full moon. Prepare to meet your doom."

Mr. Budd sniffed disparagingly when he had read the last of the notes.

"The Prophet!" he muttered contemptuously. "Some crazy fanatic, I suppose. I can't understand any sane man taking this nonsense seriously, sir."

"Neither can I," said Colonel Blair, "but there it is. Hayles may be eccentric, but he's certainly not mad, and he evidently takes these threats very seriously indeed. Tomorrow night is the night of the full moon," he added.

"And Mr. Hayles, bein' scared, wants somebody there in case this prophet feller turns up as promised," murmured the stout man.

"Exactly!" The Assistant-Commissioner helped himself to a cigarette, lit it, and nodded through the smoke.

"When d'you suggest I go, sir?" asked Mr. Budd, without enthusiasm.

"Tomorrow morning," answered Blair. "In the meanwhile, you'd better take these letters and see if you can learn anything."

The stout superintendent picked up the folder and tucked it under his arm.

"I'll take Sergeant Leek with me, sir," he said,

pausing at the door. "I don't suppose anythin' 'ull happen, but just in case it does we'd better do the thing according to routine."

He left London at ten o'clock on the following morning in his dingy little car, accompanied by the lean sergeant, and neither experienced any premonition of the tragedy that was awaiting them.

It was a hot, still morning; there was not a breath of air and the atmosphere was stifling. Neither was it appreciably cooler when they reached the open country. The sun beat down from a cloudless sky, and the surrounding countryside lay parched and scorching beneath its glare.

Liddenhurst was a tiny village with a handful of houses and a whitewashed inn. The road to the Manor House wound through dips and hollows overhung by trees, for the welcome shade of which Mr. Budd was grateful. They passed a small, square-towered church of great age with tombstones clustering closely round it, and turned into the right-hand branch of a fork. A mile farther on they came in sight of the entrance to the drive, and it was not prepossessing. The lodge was a ruin, the gates decayed structures of rotting timber.

The stout man slowed the car and eyed the faded inscription on the crumbling pillars.

"This is the place," he said, and Leek glanced dubiously at the weed-grown approach, twisting between unkempt shrubs.

"Don't look as if anybody's been here for years," he remarked, and the stout superintendent agreed.

But there was the name—readable, if only just—and he swung the car into the drive. Rounding the bend he saw before him a big, rambling house, ivy covered, and set amid a profusion of rank grass, weeds, and nettles. A great cedar tree grew in front of the porch, and in spite of the brightness of the sun its black, plate-like branches gave a sinister aspect to the place.

Mr. Budd thought it was not surprising that a man living in such a house should be troubled with nervous fancies. He began to feel a little dispirited himself.

He brought the car to a halt and got laboriously down in front of an ivy-covered porch, mounted the shallow, moss-stained steps, and pulled at a rusty iron bell. After some delay the door was opened by a thin man with a tremendous nose, who peered at him short-sightedly.

"Mr. Hayles live here?" murmured the fat detective.

"Yes, sir," said the owner of the nose. Its use was now obvious, for he talked through it. "Are you the gentleman he's expecting?"

"I'm from Scotland Yard," grunted the superintendent, and produced a card.

The large-nosed man invited him into the hall.

"If you'll wait just a moment, sir," he said nasally, "I'll tell Mr. Hayles you're here."

He took the card and hurried away up the wide stair-case. The interior of the house was in keeping with the outside. The big entrance hall was gloomy; the panelling dull and lifeless; the parquet floor worn. The musty odour, which is usually associated with houses

that have long been shut up, filled the air, and even the copper bowl of sickly-looking flowers that stood upon an old gate-legged table failed to dispel the dreariness.

Mr. Budd looked about him and mopped his perspiring forehead, wondering whether Mr. Hayles kept any beer in the house. There was a faint murmur of voices emanating from somewhere, and he had just located it as coming from behind a closed door on the right, when the servant appeared halfway down the staircase and called to him. With Leek at his heels the big man mounted the broad stairs, was conducted along a corridor, and ushered into the presence of Mr. Reuben Hayles.

The archaeologist was sitting at an enormous desk, which was littered with books and papers—an elderly, bald-headed, whiskered man, with large horn-rimmed glasses and a grey, stubbly chin.

"Sit down, Superintendent. Sit down," he said in a high-pitched, querulous voice. "I'm very glad to see you."

Mr. Budd sat down.

"This is Sergeant Leek, sir," he murmured. "I thought it best to bring him with me."

The man behind the desk nodded. He was palpably nervous. His face twitched spasmodically, and his thin hands kept moving restlessly, touching the various objects within his reach on the desk with jerky movements.

"I've seen the letters which were sent to you," said Mr. Budd, breaking a rather awkward silence. "And I

understand that you attach importance to them?"

"Do not you?" asked the old man quickly.

"To be quite candid, I don't, sir," answered the Superintendent, shaking his head. "I've seen too many such things in my time to take 'em seriously. There's a class of person who can't help writin' anonymous letters. It's a kink. It's my belief that you're just a victim of one of these queer people. That is, of course, unless you have anythin' more tangible to go on."

"No, no, I haven't!" the archaeologist broke in quickly. "I must admit, however, that these—er—communications have disturbed me, particularly in view of my recent discovery of Mohammed's tomb. Whether anything occurs tonight or not, I'm greatly relieved to have you, and—er—the sergeant on the premises. Greatly relieved!"

There was fear in the faded eyes, and Mr. Budd received the impression that Reuben Hayles knew a lot more than he had said. It was inconceivable that a man of his intelligence should have been reduced to such a state of mind merely by the receipt of those childish letters.

There was something else, something more practical that had brought that lurking fear to his eyes and induced him to apply for police protection. His thoughts were interrupted by a tap on the door and somebody came in.

"Oh, it's you, Brown!" The old man looked up over Mr. Budd's head. "Er—Superintendent. Meet my secretary, Mr. Washington Brown."

Mr. Budd turned to greet the newcomer, and suppressed a gasp of surprise.

CHAPTER TWO

THE PEOPLE OF THE MANOR HOUSE

Washington Brown bowed, smiling pleasantly, and revealing in the process a remarkably perfect set of milk-white teeth, contrasting sharply with his coal-black skin.

"I must apologise for interrupting your conference, sir," he said in faultless English. "I was unaware you had anyone with you. I have only just returned from the post office with the stamps." He came over to the desk and placed a stamp book in front of his employer.

"Thank you, Brown," murmured the archaeologist. "You didn't interrupt us. There's nothing secret about the reason for these—er—gentlemen being here." He glanced at a softly ticking clock in front of him. "Luncheon will be ready in twenty minutes, and I've no doubt they would like a wash after their journey. Will you find Murley and have them shown to their rooms?"

"Certainly, sir." The secretary went over to the door and opened it. "Will you come with me, please, gentlemen?"

Mr. Budd extricated himself from the rather close embrace of the chair in which he had been sitting, and stood up.

"Please make yourselves quite at home," said the old man. "I am extremely busy at the moment on my new book. If there's anything you want, ask Brown or Murley and they will attend to it. I will see you at luncheon." He picked up a pen and bent over his work, and they followed the secretary out into the corridor.

Closing the door softly behind him, Washington Brown murmured a polite excuse, went to the head of the stairs, and called. After a short delay, the big-nosed man appeared. He listened a little sullenly to Brown's orders, and then, when the secretary, with a smile of startling brilliancy, left them, proceeded to carry out his instructions.

The rooms that had been allotted to them were on the floor above, and commanded a view of the neglected parkland. They were large and rather drab, hung with faded chintz, and sparsely furnished. Murley pointed out a bathroom at the end of the corridor, showed them where their bags had been put, inquired if there was anything else they wanted, and took his departure.

Leek lingered in Mr. Budd's room, a lugubrioua expression on his lean face.

"Rum sort of place, ain't it?" he remarked,

The stout man grunted as he unpacked his bag. Some of the archaeologist's obvious uneasiness seemed to have communicated itself to him, or perhaps it was the atmosphere that pervaded the whole house that made

him feel vaguely conscious of a sense of impending trouble. Was there really some potent danger surrounding Reuben Hayles? Or was it only the old man's imagination?

Looked at in the setting of that dilapidated mansion with its musty smelling, disused atmosphere and unkempt grounds, the business of the anonymous threats took on a more sinister aspect. He began to wonder if anything would happen after all that night, the night on which the moon reached its full.

It was difficult to be sceptical with the memory of that fear which he had seen shining nakedly from the old man's eyes. He, at least, believed in the prophet's prophecy.

He went into the bathroom for a wash, trying vainly to shake off his sudden depression. But it remained an unpleasant feeling which refused to yield to sane thinking.

A brazen gong echoed through the house to signal the serving of lunch, and Mr. Budd, followed by the rather self-conscious and nervous Leek, went down. He was met in the hall by Murley, and conducted to the dining room.

It was a long, low-raftered room, with french windows opening on to what had, at one time, been a lawn, but which was now nothing more than a waist-high tangle of weeds and rank grass. At the long table that occupied the centre of the room, seven people were seated. The butler ushered the big superintendent and the sergeant into the two vacant chairs, and Mr.

Hayles at the head of the table introduced them to his household.

They were a queer lot of people. There was a small man of unhealthy-looking fatness, with a thick moustache and large, surprised eyes as though he lived in a constant state of astonishment at everything that was going on around him. His name Mr. Budd did not quite catch, but it sounded like Glibber. He was a cousin of Hayles', and apparently also interested in archaeology. The superintendent thought this may have accounted for his having married Mrs. Glibber, a thin, gaunt woman, with a long dark face and hollow eyes, whose age might have been anything between fifty and a hundred and twenty, so dried up and lifeless did she appear.

Next to this unpleasant-looking female was a young man with watery eyes, a pimple of a chin, and rather long, lank, fair hair that fell over his forehead every time he moved his head, and which he had a nervous habit of brushing back as though he was being bothered with flies. His name was Dinwater, and he was, apparently, their host's nephew.

On the right of the old man was a curious-looking, olive-skinned man of foreign appearance, with deep, brown, dog-like eyes, whose nationality was evidently Turkish, for he was introduced to Mr. Budd as Mahmoud Bey. And, lastly, there was the girl.

Kathleen Travers was slight and fair, and if she was not the type that a magazine artist would have used as a model for a cover design, she was pretty in a pale,

rather washed-out way. She also, the stout man discovered later, was a relation.

They eyed Mr. Budd and the lean sergeant covertly and curiously. Apparently the reason for their presence was general knowledge, for the subject of the prophet letters was brought up almost immediately and discussed at length by everybody with the exception of the girl and Washington Brown, who listened in silence.

What surprised the detective most was that they all seemed to regard the matter as serious, although nobody seemed to have the slightest inkling concerning the identity of the writer. There was also another thing which Mr. Budd's sleepy-looking eyes detected, and that was a veiled antagonism between them. They watched each other with a kind of suspicious alertness, as though each was afraid of what the other might say next.

Altogether a queer lot, the big man decided.

Sergeant Leek, embarrassed and confused by the unusual array of spoons and knives and forks beside his plate, sat in gloomy silence, eating whatever was set before him, and praying inwardly that the meal would shortly come to an end.

It did eventually, and he and Mr. Budd escaped into the weed-grown garden.

"Funny bunch, ain't they?" said Leek, shaking his head mournfully. "That girl was all right, though."

"Now don't you go gettin' sentimental," warned Mr. Budd severely.

"What d'you mean?" protested the sergeant indignantly. "I was only contrasting her with the rest of 'em."

Mr. Budd grunted and wiped his damp face. The heat was stifling, a humid, airless heat which induced a feeling of limpness. There was a haze in the sky and a tinge of copper, which he surveyed critically.

"Shouldn't be surprised if we were in for a storm," he murmured. "I should think that's what it was working up for."

"I 'ope not," said Leek anxiously. "Storms always make me feel queer."

"You're always queer!" growled Mr. Budd. "You was born queer. You must have been the queerest baby in the world!"

"I was considered a fine child—" began the sergeant.

"By the Zoological Society, I suppose," broke in the superintendent rudely, and Leek tried vainly to think of a suitable retort for this insulting remark. "Pity to let a fine place like this go to rack and ruin," went on the big man. "This must have been a garden worth seein' at one time."

They had come to the end of a bramble-lined path which led to a ramshackle summerhouse, and, turning, he eyed the old, ivy-covered building, with its quaint gables and leaded windows, a little sorrowfully, wondering why old Reuben Hayles had allowed his property to fall into such a dilapidated state.

Close to the house grew an ancient oak tree of gigantic stature, its gnarled branches almost touching the walls in some places—a majestic tree, in keeping

with its surroundings.

The rest of the day passed slowly. Tea was served in an old-fashioned drawing room, but Mr. Hayles was not present. He was working, the secretary announced, and did not wish to be disturbed.

After dinner, at which the old man looked even more nervous than he had done in the morning, he had a brief interview with Mr. Budd in the hall.

"You will make your own arrangements, Superintendent," he said, glancing quickly about him. "I shall probably be working until fairly late with my secretary."

"I'm proposin'," said the stout man, "to put Sergeant Leek on guard outside the house, and look after the inside meself."

"I sincerely hope," muttered the archaeologist, passing the tip of his tongue across his lips, "that the precautions will be unnecessary."

"I hope so too, sir," said Mr. Budd, and watched him curiously as he made his way uncertainly up the big staircase.

The sun had set in an angry bank of purple and red cloud, and when it disappeared a strange stillness settled over the countryside. Not a single leaf stirred, and there was a deep hush, as though every living thing had suddenly held its breath.

Mr. Budd got hold of Murley, and from that unprepossessing man obtained a very good idea of the layout of the house. He drew a rough plan on a page of his notebook, so that he could find his way about easily,

scribbling the names of the people who occupied the various bedrooms in their appropriate places.

Reuben Hayles slept in a room adjoining his study, and on the same floor were Professor Glibber and his wife, and Kathleen Travers. On the floor above were five bedrooms occupied respectively by Leek, Mr. Budd himself, Geoffrey Dinwater, Mahmoud Bey, and the secretary. The servants' quarters were shut off from the rest of the house by a door to which Murley alone had a key. This door was locked at night and opened in the morning, together with another door on the ground floor, which cut off the kitchen and the entire back premises.

Having primed himself with these details, Mr. Budd made a slow and ponderous round of the rooms on the ground floor, examining the window fastenings. In contrast to the rest of the house, they were new and recently fitted. It would be a clever person who could force those patent catches.

When he had completed his survey, he went in search of Leek. He found the sergeant in his room reading an evening paper, which he had borrowed from one of the servants.

"It's time you began to earn your salary," he said, glancing at his watch. "You know what you've got to do? Patrol the side of the house under Mr. Hayles' study. That'll ensure that no one can come any funny tricks that way. You understand?"

The sergeant nodded.

"What are you goin' to do?" he asked.

"I'm goin' to sit in a comfortable chair," said his superior, "in the corridor on which the study and the bedroom doors open, so that nobody can get at the old man from that direction."

Leek sighed.

"You always choose the best jobs," he grumbled. "Why can't I do that—?"

"Because I've told you to do somethin' else!" retorted Mr. Budd. "What's the use of reachin' the rank of superintendent if you can't pick the cushy jobs!"

As this was unanswerable, Leek said nothing

"Now you get along," said the big man. "If there's any disturbance, blow your whistle."

The melancholy sergeant rose gloomily to his feet. "I expect it'll all be a waste of time," he muttered. "So far as I can see, we might just as well be comfortable in our beds."

"We've come here to guard the old man," declared Mr. Budd, "and whether anythin' happens or not, we're goin' to do it! Now get along and don't argue!"

The sergeant 'got along,' and the superintendent, tucking the newspaper under his arm, went to seek the chair that he had ordered Murley to place into position for him. He found it set against the wall in the corridor, and within sight of the study door. The light that hung from the ceiling was dim, but it was sufficient to enable him to see, and he settled himself comfortably.

The drone of a voice reached his ears from behind the closed door of the room in which Mr. Hayles was working, and he concluded that the archaeologist was

dictating to his secretary.

At eleven o'clock the other members of the household began to retire for the night. Professor Glibber and his wife were the first to seek their rooms. They came along the corridor, stared curiously at the watchful Mr. Budd, muttered a curt 'good night', and disappeared through a door at the other end of the passage. After an interval, Mahmoud Bey came slowly up the stairs. He stopped at the end of the corridor, glanced along it, and continued up the second flight to the floor above. At a quarter to twelve Kathleen Travers and Geoffrey Dinwater came up the stairs together. They paused on the landing, stood talking for a moment or two, and then the girl said 'good night', and came rapidly along the passage. She gave a startled gasp as she saw Mr. Budd, and stopped.

"Oh!" she stammered. "You—you frightened me for a moment. Are you stopping here all night?"

"Most of it, I expect, miss," he answered.

"I—I hope nothing happens," she said, and he smiled.

"I don't think it will," he replied reassuringly. "I don't see very well how it can."

She wished him 'good night', and went into her room.

The voice behind the study door was still murmuring monotonously. Presently Mr. Budd heard the sound of Murley locking up, and shortly after the butler appeared.

"I've locked and bolted all the doors and fastened

the windows, sir," he said. "Is there anything further you require?"

The stout man shook his head.

"No, thank you," he answered.

"Then I'll wish you 'good night', sir," answered the butler, and went down the big staircase.

The light in the hall went out, followed by the sound of the closing and looking of the communicating door to the back premises. Mr. Budd settled himself more comfortably, took out one of his thin black cigars, and eyed it regretfully. He would have liked to smoke, but the odour would percolate to the bedrooms and possibly annoy the occupants. He put it away with a sigh, and as he did so a low rumble of thunder came to his ears. A flicker of lightning lit up the landing eerily. The storm he had predicted earlier had burst.

CHAPTER THREE
NIGHT OF THE FULL MOON

For many months afterwards Mr. Budd referred to that night at the old manor house as the first time he had ever seriously believed in the supernatural. For what eventually happened, was, by all the laws of nature, impossible.

It was one o'clock when the door of the study opened and the secretary appeared on the threshold.

"Good night, sir," he called softly as he came out, closing the door behind him.

"Mr. Hayles all right?" murmured Mr. Budd as the man came level with him.

Washington Brown nodded.

"Perfectly all right, sir," he answered, with a great display of teeth. "He's just going to bed." He wished the stout superintendent "good night" and passed on his way.

The rumble of thunder was almost continuous and getting louder. The storm was drawing nearer. Mr. Budd thought of Leek keeping his vigil in the open, and hoped he had had the forethought to provide himself with a coat. He would need it before the night

was through.

A quarter of an hour went by after the passing of the secretary, and then once again the study door opened and the old man came out into the corridor. He peered in the direction of Mr. Budd, switched out the light, shut the door, and came over to him.

"I'm going to bed now, Superintendent," he said wearily. "I trust there will be no disturbance."

"I don't think you need worry, sir," said Mr. Budd. "You can sleep quite happily. I shall be here for the rest of the night, and Sergeant Leek is outside your window. It's impossible for anyone to get near you without passin' one or other of us."

"The arrangement seems very satisfactory." The archaeologist nodded. "Good night—er—Superintendent. If there's anything you require, don't hesitate to wake Murley."

He nodded again, went over to the door adjoining that of the study, opened it, and disappeared within.

Mr. Budd yawned. He was not tired, but his vigil was a little boring. It was unlikely that anything would happen. His premonition had been the outcome of the house and its surroundings. Possibly the gathering storm, too, had played its part in producing that vague uneasiness that had grown on him throughout the day. Nothing could happen to old Hayles. The letters were just a lot of nonsense, the crazy threat of some weak-minded, religious fanatic! It was queer, though—

He was on his feet instantly as the sound reached him; a smothered exclamation, a thin scream, and the

thud of a falling body. It came from the door of the room through which a moment before the archaeologist had disappeared.

In two strides Mr. Budd had reached the portal.

"Is anythin' the matter, sir?" he called, but there was no reply.

Twisting the handle, he flung open the door and entered. A deafening crash of thunder came rolling in through the open windows simultaneously with a vivid blue-white glare. It lit the room weirdly, putting to shame the shaded lamp, and revealing with startling clearness the sprawling figure that lay on the floor. It was Reuben Hayles!

There was blood on his face and spattered on the floor around him. The front of his head was crushed in, the result of a terrible blow that must have killed him instantly. He lay in the centre of the apartment on an ancient rug.

Mr. Budd stared at him incredulously. Apart from himself and the crumpled figure, the room was empty.

Swiftly he closed the door, turned the key, and went over to the window. Another flash of violent white light split the sky and a rolling boom of thunder went reverberating over the house as he leaned out and called to Leek. The thin sergeant appeared instantly.

"Did anyone come out of this window?" snapped Mr. Budd.

"Come out of this window?" repeated the bewildered Leek. "No. Nobody ain't come out nor gone in. Why? What's 'appened?"

"Hayles has been murdered!" snarled the superintendent, but his words were drowned in another peal of thunder. "Stay where you are!" He withdrew his head as big drops of rain began to fall rapidly, went over to the body and, kneeling down, felt for the heart. There was no movement.

The old man was dead. There was no doubt of that. But how he had met his death was a mystery of mysteries,

The big man made a rapid search of the room. There was nobody concealed under the bed or in the large wardrobe, nor any sign of the weapon that must have been used to inflict such a terrible wound.

Mr. Budd rubbed his massive chin and stared about him blankly. The blow had been struck with tremendous force, and even if someone had concealed himself in the room earlier in the evening and waited for the old man to enter, it was impossible for him to have escaped. He himself had been within sight of the door all the time, and Leek was below the window. No one could have got out of that room.

He felt a little chill in the region of his spine. There was no natural explanation. What was it that had come out of the stormy night, killed, and vanished again, leaving no trace of its passage?

He shook off the superstitious fear that had momentarily taken possession of him. This was murder, and there was plenty to do. This was no time for fancies and imaginings. He made another search of the room, the vague possibility of some secret entrance crossing

his mind. It was an old house, and such things were not unknown.

But he found nothing of the kind. The floor was solid, the walls, too. There was no place for a dog to have lain concealed, let alone a human being. Yet there on the floor at his feet lay the shattered body of a man who had been killed by a savage blow; a blow that had been dealt by a powerful hand.

He went over to the window once more.

"You there, Leek?" he called. "I want you up here right away. Can you get in?"

Leek looked up pathetically through the drenching rain.

"Not unless someone lets me in," he answered.

"Well, ring the bell," said Mr. Budd. "And keep ringing till you wake the servants."

The lightning came again as the sergeant slouched away, and a thunderous detonation shook the house. Mr. Budd stared at the oak tree silhouetted against the glare, and wondered if it was possible for anyone to have swung from the window into the branches. He shook his head. It was too far away, and, anyhow, the accompanying noise would have been heard by Leek, unless—a thought occurred to him—unless the thunder had drowned it!

He wondered if he had discovered the explanation, but after a moment's consideration he saw that it was practically impossible. No man could have carried out such a feat in the time.

The muffled pealing of the bell reached his ears as

he turned back to the room. How long would Leek be before he was successful in rousing the house? Nobody as yet appeared to be aware that anything out of the ordinary had happened, or if they were, they had given no sign,

He looked down at the dead man, and his face was stern. He felt, to a certain extent, responsible. The old man had asked him for protection, and he had failed him. Yet he could have done no more than he had. He had taken what he considered were adequate precautions. They *should* have been adequate. A guard on the window, a guard on the door. It was impossible for anyone to have reached the man. And yet here was proof positive that somebody had.

He took out his handkerchief and wiped his perspiring face, and his usual sleepy expression had vanished completely.

The peeling of the bell went on monotonously. Somebody must hear it sooner or later. The local police would have to be notified, a doctor sent for, and then he saw something he had not noticed before.

The old man had fallen on his back, arms flung wide. And in one of his hands was something dark. He bent down and peered at the object, gently moved the body to get a better view, and stared in open-mouthed astonishment, for the thing which Reuben Hayles held clenched in his dead fingers was a beard of dark grey hair. And it was a false beard! The wire frame to which the hair was attached was plainly visible.

Mr. Budd straightened up, went over to the bed, and

sat down. His thoughts were chaotic, and he found it difficult to think clearly. A phrase that he had heard kept repeating itself over and over again: "The beard of the prophet. The beard of the prophet. The beard of the prophet." He had read it in books, heard it on the films. It was a commonplace oath of the East. "By the beard of the prophet." And it was the Prophet who had sent the threatening letters; the Prophet who had carried out his threat and left, leaving his beard behind.

It was insane! A nightmare! But it was true!

Mr. Budd passed a hand over his eyes wearily, almost as though he expected to find that he was dreaming. But it was no dream. There was old Reuben Hayles— dead. There in his hand was a grey beard. And here was Mr. Budd prepared to swear before any jury that nobody could have entered or left the room in which he had been killed.

The pealing of the bell stopped abruptly, and he heard voices. Presently there was a step in the corridor outside, and getting up, he walked to the door, turned the key, and opened it. Murley, a grotesque figure in a tattered dressing gown, his eyes heavy with sleep, was standing on the threshold with Leek by his side.

"What's happened?" he whispered. "What's happened?"

"Your master's been killed!" said Mr. Budd shortly. "Is there a telephone in the house?"

"Yes, sir, in the study," answered the butler, trying to catch a glimpse of the bedroom beyond the figure of the stout man. "But—but how did—?"

"I've no time to answer questions!" snapped Mr. Budd brusquely. "Telephone the nearest police station. Ask for the divisional inspector. Say that murder has been committed, and will he come here as soon as possible."

"Murder!" Murley gasped the word. "Mr. Hayles—Mr. Hayles has been murdered?"

"Yes!" snarled Mr. Budd. "Go and do as I tell you!"

The butler opened his mouth, closed it again, and hurried away. Leek, with dropped jaw and wide eyes, was staring at his superior.

"You don't mean—the old man's been killed?" he whispered incredulously.

"Didn't you hear what I told you from the window, or don't I speak plainly enough?" said Mr. Budd irritably, "If I said he was murdered, he must have been killed!"

"But—how—when?" stammered the sergeant in. coherently.

"He was killed in this room less than a quarter of an hour ago," said Mr. Budd impressively. "He was killed while you were under the window and I was outside the door! And the murderer's escaped. Now work that out!"

"But—but it's impossible," blurted Leek. "I'll swear nobody got away by the window."

"And I'll swear nobody got away by the door," growled the big man. "But Hayles is dead from a blow on the head. There's no weapon, and he's clutching a false beard in his hand. If you can explain that, you're

cleverer than I am!"

The sergeant moved forward so that he could get a view of the interior of the room, and gasped.

"Don't stand gapin' there!" said his superior. "Go along and wake the rest of the household. Explain what's happened, and take 'em down to the drawing room. Hold 'em there till I've got time to see 'em."

"But how could it have happened?" muttered the dazed Leek. "It's not possible—"

"Don't start an argument!" snarled Mr. Budd. "Just do as I tell you for once without talkin'. The only thing I can think of is that there must be some other exit from this room which we've yet to discover. Now, go along and wake those people."

The sergeant departed, and Mr. Budd once more closed and looked the door. Pulling a chair from the wall, he sat down and tried to concentrate his thoughts on the problem that had been presented to him. And it was the biggest one he had ever come up against.

Somebody had got into the room and somebody had got out, and they hadn't come either by the door or the window. So there must be another way in. In that case the mystery was less difficult. But if there was such a thing, it was very cleverly concealed. He had found no trace of it, but that didn't say it wasn't there. He realised with something of a shock that that was the first thing that had to be proved—how it was possible for the crime to have been committed. After that it would be time to seek for the murderer. But even if they were aware who had killed the old man, the

knowledge would be useless until it could be logically shown how the person had entered and left the room, the window and the door of which had been under observation at the time. No jury would convict unless that could be shown.

He heard the sound of knocking, the whispering of voices, the low cry of a woman, and guessed that Leek was carrying out instructions. Presently stumbling footsteps passed the door and faded to silence. There was a tap, and he demanded to know who was there. Murley's voice answered:

"The police are on their way, sir," said the butler. "Is there anything else I can do?"

"Wake the servants," said Mr. Budd curtly. "We shall need to question them, too."

The man went away, and the superintendent returned to his troubled thoughts. The thunder and lightning were incessant; the rain was falling in sheets. It was, he thought grimly, a fitting accompaniment for the tragedy that had taken place under his very nose.

That's what rankled. He had come to guard this man against injury, and he had failed. There would be a severe reprimand, apart from any personal feelings he might have in the matter.

His gloomy musings were interrupted presently by the sound of a car coming up the drive, and he roused himself wearily. There was work to be done; the local police had arrived.

CHAPTER FOUR
THE IMPOSSIBLE CRIME

The divisional inspector was a florid-faced, youngish-looking man, with a soft voice that seemed curiously out of place in a policeman. He was accompanied by a portly little man whom he introduced to Mr. Budd as Dr. Scavage.

"This seems to be an extraordinary business, sir," be said in hushed tones, looking down at the body after Mr. Budd had briefly explained the circumstances. "Sounds impossible to me."

"Sounds impossible to me, too!" declared the big man. "And it is impossible, the way I've described it. And yet, that's how it happened."

"Could the murderer have been hiding and slipped out while your attention was distracted?" asked Divisional Inspector Hadlow.

Mr. Budd shook his head.

"No," he answered. "He had no opportunity. From the moment I made the discovery until now I've been careful not to leave the room for a moment. There's only one sensible explanation, and that is that there's a concealed entrance somewhere."

The portly doctor, who had been making a brief examination, rose to his feet.

"He must have died instantly," he said. "I doubt if he knew what killed him."

"Can you suggest what did kill him?" asked the superintendent.

Scavage pursed his lips.

"It's a little difficult," he answered. "It was something heavy and blunt, and a great amount of force must have been used. You found no weapon in the room?"

"No," said Mr. Budd. "There was no weapon and no killer, only a body."

"But that's ridiculous!" suggested the doctor. "It's impossible for Hayles to have struck the blow himself, and even if he did, he couldn't have got rid of the weapon."

"It is ridiculous," murmured Mr. Budd. He had recovered from his first shock and was rapidly becoming more like his normal self. "It is ridiculous, and therefore it's all wrong."

"What d'you mean?" asked the police surgeon.

"I mean," explained the stout man carefully, "that if it sounds impossible and ridiculous as it happened, then it didn't happen like that at all."

"But," said the puzzled doctor, "you've just told us that it did."

"I've just told you how it appeared to have happened," answered the big man. "There's no doubt that poor feller was murdered, or that he died from a violent blow on the head which crushed his skull. Or that he died with

a false beard in his hand without anybody bein' in the room at the time. Now that's ridiculous! That's impossible! Therefore there must have been somebody in the room. But they didn't go out through the door, and they didn't go out through the window. Therefore they must have gone out somewhere else. I know that sounds a little silly, but it's logic."

"The chimney," put in Hadlow. "Have you—"

"I've examined the chimney," broke in Mr. Budd. "It's big enough, but it's got bars across. Nobody could have got in or out that way."

Dr. Scavage made an impatient gesture.

"The only thing I can suggest," he said, "is that the person must have concealed himself behind the door, waited until you'd entered the room, and then slipped out."

"And that he couldn't have done," declared Mr. Budd, "because when I opened the door I kept the handle in my hand. There was no chance of anyone slippin' by without my seein' them."

"Then there's only one explanation left," said the doctor with conviction. "There must be another entrance."

Hadlow had brought a sergeant and constable with him. The sergeant was called up. Mr. Budd, the divisional inspector, and this man made a meticulous search of every inch of the apartment, but no trace or sign of any secret door or an opening in the walls or ceiling could they discover. No possible way by which the killer could have entered or left the room. The

house was well built, the walls were eighteen inches thick, and the whole room was as solid as a bank vault. The door and window offered the only way of exit or entrance. Yet the murderer could have used neither. His coming and going was an impenetrable mystery.

"Well, that's that!" said Mr. Budd wearily. "We've established one thing, anyway."

"We've established an impossibility, sir," pointed out Hadlow.

Dr. Scavage, who had been watching with interest, uttered an exclamation.

"Look here," he said suddenly, "the window was open, wasn't it, when you made the discovery?"

"It was," admitted the big man.

"Well, couldn't something have been catapulted or thrown from outside?"

It was Hadlow who shook his head.

"If that had been the case, doctor," he said, "the thing would be here."

"Yes, that's true," said Scavage disappointedly.

"Apart from which," remarked Mr. Budd, "it would have taken some force to have thrown anything large enough to have inflicted that wound. No, I don't think that's how it was done."

He walked thoughtfully over to the window and looked out. The storm was still raging. At intermittent intervals the park and the surrounding country were lit up by the lightning, and the rolling peals of thunder followed one another in quick succession.

"I'm wondering," he said, "if that tree could have

had anything to do with it?"

Hadlow was an intelligent man and grasped his meaning quickly.

"You mean could the murderer have reached the window from the tree and got back the same way?" he said.

Mr. Budd nodded.

"I don't see how," said the divisional inspector. "It's a good fifteen feet away. I don't see how anyone could have bridged the gap."

"Well, then, I give it up," murmured Mr. Budd despairingly. "This 'ull go down on record as the first crime to have been committed by an invisible man. An invisible man wearin' a false beard," he added. "It's insane!"

CHAPTER FIVE
MR. BUDD MEETS THE PROPHET

The body of the dead man was covered with a sheet but otherwise left exactly as it had been found. It could not be moved until after the police photographs had been taken, and this would have to wait until the morning. The window was closed and latched and the door locked, and when Mr. Budd had put the key in his pocket he went down, accompanied by the divisional inspector, to interview the people of the household, leaving the local sergeant on guard in the corridor.

The storm was still raging with unabated fury. The rain hissed and splashed and the thunder roared and boomed, filling the night with a deafening clamour.

Murley was in the hall talking to a stolid-looking constable when they reached the foot of the stairs, and he came over as soon as he saw the big man.

"The servants are all up, sir," he said in a low voice. "They're all in the kitchen, if you want to see them."

"I'll see 'em presently," said Mr. Budd, and went over to the door of the drawing room.

There was no sound from within, and turning the handle he entered. The six occupants were grouped

in uneasy silence round the fireplace, and Leek, who was sitting uncomfortably on the edge of a chair near the door, looked up with relief when they came in. Mr. Budd paused for a moment on the threshold, sleepily eyeing the sketchily attired assemblage, before he shut the door behind him and advanced further into the room.

It was Geoffrey Dinwater who was the first to speak.

"Is it true—about Uncle Reuben?" he demanded, blinking nervously.

"I'm afraid it is, sir," answered the stout superintendent. "Mr. Hayles is dead!"

A variety of expressions crossed the staring faces before him, a whole gamut of emotions ranging from fear to incredulity.

"How—?" The secretary began the question and stopped.

"He was murdered," said Mr. Budd bluntly.

Kathleen Travers caught her breath with a queer, gasping sound, and her face went white to the lips. Mahmoud Bey remained silent, but his eyes fastened themselves on Mr. Budd in an unwavering and rather disconcerting atare. Glibber clicked his teeth, and his habitually astonished face was so ludicrous that the big man felt an almost uncontrollable desire to laugh. Mrs. Glibber stared at the empty grate, her face devoid of any emotion whatever. The girl cleared her throat huskily.

"I—I can't believe it," she muttered unsteadily. "How did it happen? Who killed him?"

"That's what I'd like to know, miss," said the fat detective. "I'd very much like to know who killed him—and how!"

"How?" Glibber repeated the word in a questioning tone. "D'you mean that you don't know the cause of death?"

"No, sir," answered Mr. Budd. "I don't mean that at all. I know the cause of death all right—there's nothin' mysterious about that."

"Then what do you mean, Superintendent?" The soft voice of Mahmoud Bey asked the question.

"I'll tell you what I mean, sir," said Mr. Budd, and proceeded to do so.

They listened to what he had to say in amazement.

"But—but—" protested Geoffrey Dinwater, when he had finished. "It's not possible."

The big man sighed wearily.

"We've all said that," he murmured. "And the answer is, it happened!"

"There are more things in Heaven and earth than the mind of man dreams of," misquoted Mrs. Glibber suddenly and surprisingly.

"Meanin', ma'am," said the superintendent, turning towards her, "that Mr. Hayes was killed by somethin' supernatural?"

"There is no other explanation," declared the woman with conviction.

"Nonsense, Annabel!" said her husband severely. "To the scientific mind there is no such thing as the supernatural."

She shot him an angry glance and shrugged her thin shoulders.

"Perhaps you can offer a better explanation," she sneered—and there was a meaning in her voice that made the detective open his eyes sharply.

"Well," remarked the stout man, "I can't say I know enough about the supernatural to argue, ma'am. But a spook in a false beard doesn't sound convincin' to me."

"The idea," squeaked Glibber, "is preposterous—completely preposterous!" He waved it out of existence with a gesture. "There must be some practical explanation."

"If you can think of one, I'd very much like to hear it," murmured Mr. Budd. "In the meanwhile, I should like to ask one or two questions, if you don't mind."

"What kind of questions?" murmured Mahmoud Bey softly.

"All sorts," answered the stout superintendent. "F'rinstance, did any of you hear anythin' unusual between half past twelve and one?"

"How could we?" snapped Mrs. Glibber. "We were all in bed and asleep!"

"I wasn't asleep," said Dinwater. "The thunder woke me. But I heard nothing—nothing unusual."

"Nor I," said Washington Brown.

"And you, Miss Travers?" asked Mr. Budd, and the girl shook her head.

"Nor me," put in Mahmoud Bey softly.

It was merely a routine question, and the big man had expected a negative result. If he himself and the

watchful Leek had heard nothing, it was unlikely that any of these people would. He cleared his throat.

"Now, regardin' these Prophet letters," he went on. "Mr. Hayles took them more seriously than they seemed to warrant, and I am under the impression that he had a reason for that which he didn't disclose. Can anybody tell me what that reason was?"

There was a silence as he looked from one to the other, and then Washington Brown moved restlessly.

"Yes," said Mr. Budd inquiringly,"what is it?"

"I don't know whether I ought to tell you"—the secretary was hesitant—"Mr. Hayles expressly asked me not to mention it in case it should prejudice you. He had a strong suspicion who sent those letters."

"Oh, he did, eh?" Mr. Budd was interested. "And who did he think sent them?"

"A neighbour—a man who lives in Liddenhurst," answered the secretary. "He and Mr. Hayles have had several quarrels. He's a religious fanatic, and he thought that Mr. Hayles' profession was sacrilegious."

"Do you mean the queer man?" broke in Inspector Hadlow.

Washington Brown nodded.

"Yes, that's the fellow."

Mr. Budd turned quickly.

"Who is this queer man you're talkin' about?" he demanded.

"He's a peculiar chap," said the divisional inspector. "He lives in a cottage on the outskirts of the village. His name's Daniel Thane. But everybody calls him the

'Queer Man' in the district. He's a little bit touched, I think."

"H'm!" commented the stout superintendent. "And Mr. Hayles was under the impression that these anonymous letters came from him, eh?" He addressed the secretary, and Brown nodded. "Why didn't he say so?" demanded Mr. Budd.

"Well, he wasn't sure," replied Washington Brown. "It was only because he'd had trouble with Thane before that he thought they might have come from him. But if his suspicions were wrong, he didn't want to get the chap into trouble."

"I've seen the man you're talking about," put in Geoffrey Dinwater—"tall, lean fellow. Goes about in sandals and a robe."

"That's the man, sir," said Inspector Hadlow. "Eccentric, but I've always thought he was harmless."

"Maybe he is," remarked Mr. Budd. "On the other hand, maybe he isn't. Though I don't see how anyone, harmless or otherwise, got in and out of that room. Still, we ought to see him. How far away is this cottage?"

"About a couple of miles," said Hadlow.

The superintendent looked at his watch.

"Gettin' on for three," he murmured. "I'd like to find out whether this feller's sleepin' or what he's doing." He came to a sudden decision. "We'll go along there. You can stay here, Leek. The rest of you can go back to your rooms. I'll see you in the mornin'. Nobody's to leave the house—understand that!"

He went out into the hall, followed by Hadlow, and

beckoned to Murley, who was still lurking uneasily about.

"You can send the servants to bed," he said. "I haven't got time to see 'em now, and they'd better try and get some sleep."

"Don't you think," ventured Hadlow, "we ought to leave seeing Thane until the morning?"

"No, I don't," said Mr. Budd. "I want to see him now. I want to know what he was doin' at the time Hayles was killed."

He pulled open the massive front door and stared out into the rain-drenched night. The thunder was still muttering and rumbling, and the lightning played fitfully over the neglected grounds. With a resigned shrug of his shoulders the divisional inspector followed him to the waiting car and climbed up behind the wheel. Mr. Budd took his place beside him, and they drove off through the rain.

Except for the intermittent flashes of lightning the night was pitch-dark. There might be a full moon somewhere, but there was no sign of it, and the heavy thunderclouds shut out even the faint light that might have come from the stars.

The car hissed and splashed and bumped along the narrow road, the windscreen wiper working furiously, and the headlights glittering on the downpour, so that the falling drops, as they came within their rays, looked like little globules of molten fire.

They sped through the sleeping village, ascended a steep hill, the wheels skidding and sliding, and came

to a halt at the entrance to a footpath between a tangle of briars.

"We'll have to walk from here," grunted the inspector. "It's too narrow to take the car up."

Mr. Budd got silently down and waited for Hadlow to join him. The inspector led the way along the narrow, winding track that passed through a dark coppice, and presently ended altogether in front of a tiny building, which was set in an oblong of garden. It was very small, and the big man drew in his breath quickly as he saw a glimmer of light shining dimly from behind a latticed window.

Hadlow led the way to a gate, opened it, and walked up a cinder path to the creeper-covered porch. A vivid flash of lightning illumined the scene, and Mr. Budd saw that the garden was full of old-world flowers that in daylight must have been a blaze of colour.

Hadlow reached the porch, and raising his fist, hammered on the door. There was a movement within, a shuffling step on bare boards became audible, and then the door was jerked open and the tall figure of a man, holding a lamp, peered out at them.

"Who comes at this hour?" said a deep voice. "What do you want?"

"We'd like to have a word with you, Mr. Thane," said Mr. Budd before Hadlow had time to reply. "Mr. Reuben Hayles has been murdered!"

A pair of dark, hollow eyes turned on him.

"When did it happen?" asked a deep voice.

"Shortly before half-past one this morning,"

answered the superintendent.

"Then the prophecy has been fulfilled," said the strange man. "Mohammed has struck down the desecrator of his grave! The vengeance of the prophet has fallen upon him!"

Never in his life before had the stout superintendent had such an extraordinary experience. There was something unreal, unnatural, about the whole situation. The thin, wild-looking figure of the man with the lamp, framed in the cottage doorway, the rumbling of the thunder, and the incessant flickering of the lightning, the monotonous hissing splash of the rain and the deep voice, were like the component parts of some nightmare.

Hadlow must have felt something of the same sensation, for he seemed at a loss. It was Daniel Thane who broke the silence that followed on his last speech.

"Are you friends of Reuben Hayles?" he demanded, and Mr. Budd jerked himself out of the spell that had fallen over him.

"No," he answered. "We represent the police."

"The police?" repeated the queer man, and there was no sign of apprehension either in his voice or face. "Why, then, have you come to me?"

"Mr. Hayles," said the fat detective, "received several letters threatenin' him. From information received, we're under the impression that you wrote them."

"Supposing that to be true, what then?" asked Daniel Thane.

"Then," said Mr. Budd shortly, "I should like an

account of your movements between half-past twelve and half-past one this mornin'."

"Are you labouring under the delusion," said the queer man, "that I am responsible for the death of this man, Hayles?"

"I don't know what I'm labourin' under," said the stout superintendent irritably. "But I want to know what you were doin', all the same."

"I had no hand in Hayles' death," said Daniel Thane, "but I read it in the stars and in the music of the breeze. He died because he had violated the tomb of the prophet."

"That may be," said Mr. Budd. "But somebody killed him."

"The hand of Mohammed killed him," declared the queer man. "It was written that Reuben Hayles should die, and he died." He drew himself up, his gaunt figure in its curious monkish robe looking strangely digni-fied in the flickering light of the lamp. "For the sake of knowledge, for the sake of worldly power and prestige, he violated sacred things. You tell me he is dead, and I am not surprised. Let others take heed and walk in the paths of righteousness and humility."

"That doesn't answer my question," said Mr. Budd stubbornly. "I asked you what you were doin' between half-past twelve and half-past one!"

"I was out," replied Daniel Thane. "When the moon is at its full, the spirits are abroad. The ancient goddess of Isis dances with Thor on such a night, and the souls of men can rise above the trivialities of mundane things

and commune with the glories of nature."

"Crazy as a coot!" murmured Mr. Budd below his breath, and looked a little helplessly at Hadlow.

He had dealt with all sorts of strange people during his long career, but Daniel Thane was completely outside his experience.

"During the time you were out did you go anywhere near the Manor House?" asked the divisional inspector, in an endeavour to answer the mute appeal in his confrère's eyes.

"Why should you question where I went?" demanded the queer man. "Is not the country free to all who would enjoy its changing moods?"

"There's certain laws of property," said the big man.

"I violate no laws!" retorted Daniel Thane. "Neither the laws of man nor the laws of nature. But if you would speak further with me, come inside. My habitation is open to all men who are heavy laden."

Mr. Budd was inclined to take this as a subtle reference to his stoutness, but he followed the other into the narrow passage, glad to get out of the rain, which was trickling coldly down his back.

The floor was bare of covering, but scrupulously clean, and the queer man led them into a room on the right. Here, also, was neither carpet nor linoleum, but the boards had been scrubbed to a whiteness that was dazzling. There was scarcely any furniture. A plain deal-topped table stood in the centre, and beside it a chair. Against one wall had been built a row of book-shelves, also of plain wood, containing several battered

volumes. On another table near the window, rather to the big man's surprise, stood an ancient typewriter.

The sight of it set any doubts he might have had at rest. Old Reuben Hayles's suspicions had been correct. The letters that had so alarmed him had come from this strange individual who had set the lamp down on the centre table and was regarding them gravely.

"You are looking at my typewriter," he said suddenly. "A present from my niece, and an instrument that has been of inestimable value to me in my studies."

"Very useful things," said Mr. Budd. "So you did write those letters to Mr. Hayles?"

"Why should I deny it?" answered Daniel Thane. "I knew that death was coming to him, and I warned him. I could do no more."

"How did you know?" The superintendent adopted a conversational tone.

"It was revealed to me," said the queer man. "I was vouchsafed a vision."

"But why did you send them anonymously?" inquired the fat detective. "And post 'em in London?"

"Because I did not wish Hayles to know they emanated from me," answered the other. "Had he been aware of the source he would have ignored them. He was a self-willed, obstinate man."

"You often go to London?" asked the superintendent.

"I go occasionally to visit my niece who works in a large store," said Daniel Thane. "I did not anticipate that my warnings would have any effect, but I hoped

that they might prepare Reuben Hayles for the doom that was inevitable."

Mr. Budd gently rubbed his chin. He was in something of a quandary. He lacked sufficient evidence to arrest this man for the crime, even had he believed him guilty, which he did not. To do so would necessitate endowing him with supernatural powers. But at least his visit had resulted in something. He had discovered the origin of the letters, and the discovery had satisfied him about one thing, and the new possibilities it gave rise to surprised and puzzled him. He wanted time to consider this extraordinary case from the fresh angle that his discovery had suggested.

In some respects it was alarming, and the problem how anyone got in or out of Reuben Hayles's bedroom was still unsolved. But it offered fresh material to work on.

There was nothing to be done with Daniel Thane at this stage of the inquiry, and they took their leave of that strange man. He accompanied them courteously to the door, and here Mr. Budd put his last question.

"Why did you sign those letters 'the Prophet'?" he asked casually.

The queer man surveyed him haughtily.

"Because," he said gravely. "I am a direct descendant of Mohammed!"

He watched them until they reached the gate, and then closed the door.

"Well, what do you make of that?" said Hadlow, as they set off to return to the car.

"The poor feller's barmy!" answered the big man briefly.

"I know that!" The divisional inspector was a little impatient. "I mean do you think he's guilty of Hayles's murder?"

Mr. Budd shook his head.

"No, I don't think he's guilty," he declared. "He wrote those letters, and he certainly had a hand in the killing of Hayles, but I don't think he's guilty of murder."

"You mean he's mad, and therefore not responsible for his actions?" said Hadlow. "But still, I don't see—"

"That's true, but it isn't what I meant," answered Mr. Budd cryptically.

And all the way back to the Manor House the divisional inspector tried to discover some sense out of this contradictory assertion, without success. If ever Hadlow had been relieved to have a murder investigation taken out of his hands, it was now.

CHAPTER SIX
FIND THE MOTIVE

The storm ended with the coming of daylight, and dawn brought a clear sky and the prospect of a fine day. The police photographers arrived just after it was light, and for some little while there was the popping of magnesium flares in the death-room, and the acrid odour of burnt powder.

When they had gone, the body of the archaeologist was removed to a waiting ambulance and taken to the mortuary to await the inquest. Divisional Inspector Hadlow went back to the station to make his report, and Mr. Budd, accompanied by the melancholy and yawning Leek, went out into the sunshine for a tour of inspection.

He satisfied himself that the oak tree grew too far away from the house for anyone, however active, to have used it as it means of reaching the study window. Neither was there any means by which the wall could have been scaled. There was no ivy here, and nothing that offered a hand or foothold.

"I keep tellin' yer," protested Leek wearily, as he watched his superior conduct this examination, "that

nobody could 'ave come this way! I was within a few yards of the place the 'ole time, and I'd 'ave 'eard 'em!"

"You may have been in a trance!" grunted Mr. Budd.

"You've never found me neglectin' me duty!" said Leek indignantly. "I was as alert last night as I am at midday!"

"Then I should think a regiment of soldiers could have come by you and you wouldn't 'ave noticed 'em!" retorted Mr. Budd unkindly.

The long-suffering sergeant sighed.

"You will 'ave your little joke," he said aggrievedly. "But seriously, I tell yer, no one could 'ave come this way without me seein' 'em."

The big man was prepared to believe it. He went in from his fruitless search and interviewed the servants, but he learned nothing. The rest of the household were not up, and after an early breakfast he settled himself in the drawing room to consider the position.

He felt certain that so far as the anonymous letters were concerned, they could be eliminated. They had, in his opinion, nothing to do with the death of old Reuben Hayles beyond suggesting it to the murderer. That was the new angle that had occurred to him during his interview with the queer man. Daniel Thane had sent those letters purely as the outcome of a delusion, and the person who had killed the archaeologist had seized upon them as a screen behind which he or she could carry out their crime. At least, that was the theory that Mr. Budd was working on.

Daniel Thane might be crazy, but he was not a killer.

The big man could not imagine him killing anyone, much less could he imagine him wandering about in a false beard. That, he felt, was the crux of the whole business.

He had examined the beard carefully, and discovered that it was not even made of real hair. It was a very bad beard; the kind of trumpery thing that one uses at Christmas. It would have been obviously false if anyone had worn it. And yet the murderer had worn it, and the old man had, apparently, torn it off just before he died. There was no other way to account for its being found in his hand.

Discarding the letters as having any bearing on the archaeologist's death brought up a fresh question. What was the motive? Originally it seemed that he had been hailed by some crazy fanatic because he had violated the tomb of Mohammed. But according to Mr. Budd's new theory this didn't still hold good. Therefore, he had been killed for some other reason. What was it? If he could discover the motive, then the identity of the murderer shouldn't be difficult, and that brought him once more to the principal problem. How had the crime been carried out?

It was useless finding the murderer until he could explain that. The killer could afford to snap his fingers. "You say," Mr. Budd could hear him remarking triumphantly, "that I killed Hayles. Prove it! Show how it was possible, in the circumstances, for anybody to have killed him!"

And that was his strong suit. Until that could be

answered satisfactorily he was safe—safe even though everyone in the world knew him to be guilty.

The big man threw away the butt of the cigar he had been smoking and lighted another. What had promised to be a very boring business had turned out to be remarkably interesting. Someone had taken advantage of the threatening letters for their own purpose; had even made a profitable use of the presence of Mr. Budd himself. Behind the murder of the old man was a cunning brain, and the stout superintendent, the more he thought of it, the more uneasy he became. The pattern was not yet complete. At the back of his mind he had an unpleasant feeling that there was more to come—that this killing of the archaeologist was only an item in the scheme which had been hatched by the unknown.

However, his visit to Daniel Thane had led to something. He was no longer hampered by those anonymous letters. He might have wasted a lot of time on them. Now he was free to devote his inquiries elsewhere.

Just before lunch Reuben Hayles's solicitor arrived. He was a jovial, red-faced man, not in the least like the usual conception of a lawyer. The stout man learned that Washington Brown had telephoned for him.

"This is a dreadful thing—a terrible thing!" he said, when Mr. Budd had a private interview with him. "Have you any idea who could have been responsible for the poor old fellow's death?"

The big man shook his head.

"Not at the moment, but I'm rather glad you're here,

though, because you may be able to help me."

Mr. Kinman looked at him in mild surprise.

"In what way?" be demanded.

"Well, I'm anxious," explained Mr. Budd, "to discover a motive, and the most likely motive is money. Was Mr. Hayles a rich man?"

"It depends," said the cautious lawyer, "what you consider a rich man. Reuben Hayles was very well off. Everything considered, I suppose he was worth about two hundred thousand pounds."

Mr. Budd whistled softly.

"I'd call that almost a millionaire," he murmured. "Who gets all this money, sir?"

The solicitor smiled and shook his head.

"I'm afraid that's not going to help you," he said. "Everything goes to his niece, Miss Travers, and I don't think you could suspect her."

Mr. Budd scratched his chin.

"No, I don't think I can, sir," he admitted. "Not because she's a girl and pretty, but because this crime was carried out by somebody more powerful. I doubt if she'd have the strength to administer a blow like what killed Mr. Hayles. So she gets all the money, does she?"

"Yes. I have the will with me," replied Mr. Kinman.

"And did she know she was goin' to get it?" asked the fat detective.

The lawyer shook his head.

"No, she had no idea!" he declared. "The only people who knew were myself, Mr. Hayles, and the secretary, Brown."

"H'm!" said the big man disappointedly. "Well I don't think that's goin' to help me a lot. Had Mr. Hayles any enemies?"

"Every man has enemies," retorted the solicitor sententiously. "But I know of no one who hated Hayles so much that they would wish to kill him."

And on this unsatisfactory note the interview ended.

The big man had to admit that he was completely at sea. With the exception of the beard, he had no clue at all to the identity of the killer. Neither could he find a motive, which might have given him a pointer.

What was the reason behind the old man's death? He had exhausted money, and vengeance seemed unlikely. What remained? Jealousy?

He rambled about the neglected grounds after lunch, smoking cigar after cigar, irritable and depressed, and he was coming despondently back to the house with the intention of going to his room for a short rest, when he saw Murley looking anxiously about. The butler caught sight of him at the same moment, and came quickly towards him.

"I've been trying to find you, sir," he said, and his face was drawn and worried. "I've found something important."

"What is it?" asked Mr. Budd hopefully.

"If you'll come with me, I'll show you, sir," said the big-nosed man, and led the way into the house.

He ascended the staircase, passed along the corridor in which Mr. Budd, on the previous night, had kept his vigil, and paused outside a door at the far end.

"This is Miss Travers' room," he whispered. "She's downstairs in the drawing room at the moment. Come in." He turned the handle softly, entered, and waited for the stout Superintendent to join him. "This is what I wanted to show you, sir," he said in the same low tone.

Going over to a wardrobe he opened it, pulled aside some dresses that were hanging neatly on hangers, and pointed. Mr. Budd stooped and peered in the direction of his finger. On the bottom shelf of the wardrobe were a number of shoes, but it was not these that caught his eye and riveted his attention. It was a square, iron weight that bore on the side a large 3, followed by the letters lbs.

A three-pound weight that was covered with blood!

CHAPTER SEVEN
SUSPECTS NARROWED DOWN

Mr. Budd stared at the sinister object for a second or two without speaking, then he looked at Murley.

"How did you come to find this?" he asked.

The butler passed the tip of his tongue over his dry lips.

"The cook missed it, sir," he said. "It's usually kept in the kitchen. We use it as a doorstop. The door between the kitchen and the scullery is badly hung, and unless you have something to prevent it, it swings to of its own accord. Very inconvenient it is when you're busy and in a hurry. We looked for it, but we couldn't find it anywhere, although it had been there yesterday. It was Milly, the housemaid, who discovered it here. Miss Travers had spilt some grease on a pair of white shoes, and she gave them to Milly to try to get it off. When she came to put them back, she saw this and noticed the blood. She was scared and frightened, and told me. I made sure she hadn't been imagining things, and came to find you, sir."

"Did she touch it?" asked Mr. Budd sharply.

The butler shook his head.

"I asked her that," he said, "thinking of fingerprints." He smiled faintly. "I read a lot of detective stories in my spare time," he explained. "Never imagined that I'd have a crime on my own doorstep, so to speak."

"H'm!" grunted Mr. Budd. "You haven't mentioned it to anybody else?"

"No, sir. Only the servants know, of course."

"Well, go down and tell 'em to say nothing," said the big man sharply.

"You don't think—?" The butler hesitated. "You don't think Miss Travers could have—?"

"I don't think anythin'!" broke in Mr. Budd untruthfully, for he was thinking lots of things and very rapidly. "Go and do as I tell you."

Murley departed rather reluctantly, and when he had gone, the stout superintendent gingerly lifted the weight out of the wardrobe by the crossbar at the top. There was a magazine on the table by the bed, and this he brought over, placed it on the top of a dressing table by the window, and stood the weight on it.

There was no doubt that this was the weapon that had struck that terrible blow which had killed old Reuben Hayles. The blood had dried, and in it were several grey hairs. And it had been found in Kathleen Travers's wardrobe.

He frowned at it, rubbing his massive chin. The girl had had the motive, but it was impossible to imagine that she could have had strength enough to wield such a heavy thing. Impossible to imagine it even if she could explain how she had done it.

His mind went back to the previous night. He remembered her passing him in the passage and going into her room. She had not come out again. How, if she was guilty, had she succeeded in committing the murder?

Back once more, he thought grimly, at the old problem. How? How? How?

Was it possible there did exist some means of communication between this and Hayles's bedroom? Some other entrance than the door and the window?

Mechanically he shook his head. It was impossible! If there had been anything of the sort, the careful inspection that they had made would have revealed it. No, if Kathleen Travers was responsible for the death of her uncle, she had planned the crime with superhuman ingenuity, planned it so well that it was impossible to conjecture how she had done it.

He tore the middle out of the magazine and carefully wrapped the weight on it. The girl would have to explain how that incriminating object had got where it had been found.

He came out of the room softly, closed the door, and walked rapidly along the corridor. On the landing he met Geoffrey Dinwater coming up the stairs.

"Hello!" said that vacuous young man. "How are things going? Have you discovered anything?"

"Well, we're followin' up a line of inquiry," said Mr. Budd evasively. "But we've got nothin' definite yet."

"How did you get on with old Thane?" asked Dinwater.

"He's a queer fellow," replied the big man. "But I

don't think there's any harm in him."

"He's queer enough," remarked the other. "Got religious mania, or something. He came here once, and there was a devil of a row. Tried to show uncle the error of his ways. Said that all this opening of graves was sacrilegious, and that vengeance would certainly overtake him if he continued."

"He talked like that when I saw him," said Mr. Budd. "But he's loony! I'd like a word with you, Mr. Dinwater, in private."

The young man raised his eyebrows.

"Come up to my room," he said. "I was just going to do a little work."

Mr. Budd followed him up to the second landing and into a room at the beginning of the corridor, similar to the one below. It was an extremely untidy appartment, but more comfortably furnished than the other bedroom. An easy chair was drawn up near the grate, and a large table littered with books and papers stood in the window.

"I'm rather keen on mathematics," said Dinwater, waving his hand towards the table.

"And on detective fiction, apparently, sir," remarked Mr. Budd, eyeing a bookcase that was stuffed with a number of crime novels.

Dinwater smiled.

"That's my relaxation," he said. "You've got to have something after a course of higher mathematics. What did you want to see me about?"

"I take it," said Mr. Budd slowly, "that you live here

permanently?"

The other nodded.

"Yes, that's right," he said. "Both Kathleen and I. Our mothers were Uncle Reuben's sisters. They're both dead now. The old man was very decent, he sort of adopted us."

"I see," murmured Mr. Budd. "And you were always on friendly terms with him?"

Dinwater eyed him keenly.

"Look here," he said, "what's the idea behind these questions?"

"Nothing, sir," said Mr. Budd soothingly. "Just that I want to acquire all the information I can."

"Well, yes," said the other. "Uncle was a little eccentric, but we got on with him fairly well. He was away a lot, of course."

"There was no trouble at all?" persisted the stout man.

"Why? Why do you ask that?" asked Dinwater sharply. "Has somebody been talking? There was nothing in that. I dare say uncle would have come round in time."

Mr. Budd had no idea to what he referred, but he thought it best not to appear ignorant.

"You think he would?" he said doubtfully.

"Of course he would. He had nothing against the man. It was only that I think he was under the impression Kathleen was too young to consider marriage."

The fat detective felt a sudden quickening of his pulses. Here was something! But it had to be handled

carefully or Dinwater as a source of information would dry up.

"Well, maybe he was right," he said.

"I don't know," replied Dinwater frowning. "She's of age, and surely entitled to choose her own husband."

"It depends upon the choice," said Mr. Budd.

The other nodded.

"I believe you're right," he said. "I think that had a lot to do with the trouble. Uncle was queer and old-fashioned in many ways. He thought Tinsdale wasn't— well, rich enough!"

Now, who's this feller Tinsdale? thought Mr. Budd.

"A doctor, especially a newcomer, hasn't got much chance of a practice in Liddenhurst," went on Dinwater. "Although I think Arthur Tinsdale's a clever fellow, and will make his way in the world. Who told you about the quarrel?"

"I heard of it," said the big man evasively.

"That old cat, Annabel, I'll bet!" grunted Geoffrey Dinwater. "The scandal-mongering old busybody! She made it worse by butting in and siding with uncle. That's really what got Kathleen all worked up." He lit a cigarette and flung the match into the grate. "You can take it from me," he said, "that that's got nothing to do with uncle's death. Kathleen's got a temper, but she doesn't mean half she says. You'll find this fellow Daniel Thane's at the bottom of the whole business."

"Well, I shall be very glad to find someone at the bottom of the business," remarked Mr. Budd wearily. "At the present moment I don't see any bottom to it at

all."

"No, it's a pretty ticklish problem," said Dinwater. "I've puzzled over it a lot. The difficulty is, of course, how the murderer escaped."

"And how he got in," supplemented the fat man. "Yes that's the difficulty, Mr. Dinwater. Maybe you can work it out mathematically?"

The other looked at him seriously.

"Maybe I can," he said.

"Well, if you do, you might let me know," said Mr. Budd, and took his departure.

He had learned something fresh and something important. There had been a quarrel between Kathleen Travers and her uncle over a doctor, Tinsdale, who, apparently, had a practice in Liddenhurst. Old Reuben Hayles had obviously objected to the marriage of these two. And Tinsdale was penniless.

Here was a further motive for the girl to wish her uncle out of the way. With Hayles dead, she became the possessor of a large fortune, and the freedom to marry the man she wanted to. It was a strong motive, and coupled with that blood-stained weight, Milly, the maid, had discovered at the bottom of her wardrobe, was sufficient, in any ordinary circumstances, to warrant an arrest. But, and here Mr. Budd swore softly below his breath, but—how had she managed to do the impossible? And why had that false beard been found in the dead man's hand?

It was incredible to suppose that the girl had worn a beard, not only incredible but ludicrous. The big man

had a strong sense of humour, and in his mind's eye he could visualise Kathleen Travers with that atrociously obvious false beard. It was ridiculous!

All the same, she had the motive, and the weapon had been found in her room. A thought struck him. Was it possible that this Doctor Tinsdale was guilty?

Had he been the wearer of the beard? Were he and the girl in it together?

This was probable. It was more than probable, if—and again the big man swore gently to himself—if it could be found how he had managed to do the impossible.

CHAPTER EIGHT
MR. BUDD WORKS IT OUT

The divisional inspector called after tea to inform Mr. Budd that the inquest had been fixed for the Tuesday morning, and to the astonished Hadlow, the big man related the further discoveries he had made.

"It looks pretty serious for the girl," commented the inspector when he had finished. "I know this man Tinsdale. Quite a respectable, hard-working young fellow. When he's got any work to do," he added. "He bought old Withers's practice when he died. But I should think he was pretty nearly at the end of his tether. Most of the patients in the neighbourhood had only kept on with Withers out of sentimental reasons, and they were only too anxious of the excuse to go over to Johns. This place isn't really big enough for two doctors, and Johns gets all the plums. I happen to know that Tinsdale owes money right and left. There's certainly motive enough there, considering the money the girl'll come into now Hayles is dead."

"There's motive enough," said Mr. Budd irritably. "It isn't that that's worrying me, Hadlow. It's the method."

The inspector nodded.

"Yes, that's the stumbling block, sir," he agreed. "I've thought and thought until my head aches, but I can't see any explanation."

"That's where our hands are tied," muttered Mr. Budd. "We can't do anythin', Hadlow. We can't arrest anybody until we can explain how they could have killed the old man. There must be somethin' we've overlooked."

"I suppose"—the divisional inspector was a little diffident—"I suppose your sergeant didn't fall asleep, or anything?"

"No. I can vouch for him," said the stout superintendent—an assertion that would have gratified Sergeant Leek immensely had he been there to hear. "If he says nobody came by the window, nobody did! Apart from which, I must have been in the room three seconds after the blow was struck. And the first thing I did was to go to the window. I should have seen anybody!"

Hadlow shrugged his shoulders.

"Well, there it is," he said dubiously. "Somebody killed the old man, and they killed him with that weight. I suppose Dr. Scavage's suggestion isn't feasible at all?"

"You mean that it was flung through the window?" said Mr. Budd, and shook his bead. "How far d'you think you could throw a three-pound weight, Hadlow? And how are you goin' to get it back again after you've thrown it?"

"It might have had a string attached to it, or something like that?" suggested the inspector, but again Mr. Budd shook his head. "You try pullin' a three-pound

weight out of an open window by a piece of string," he said. "It would have fallen on the floor, and you've got to pull it up over the sill. It couldn't be done."

"Well, it's the only thing I can think of," sighed Hadlow, "unless"—he smiled a little wanly—"that woman downstairs—Mrs. Gibber—was right, and it's something more than the mind of man dreams of."

"Bosh!" said the stout man crossly. "Don't you go gettin' all spiritualistic and psychic. There's a natural explanation, same as there is to anythin', if we can only find it."

"If we can only find it!" echoed Hadlow dubiously.

Mr. Budd rose to his feet with an unaccustomed access of energy, and his fist came down heavily on the table.

"We've got to find it, and we're goin' to find it!" he declared. "There's nothin' that happens that isn't possible of an explanation, and this has happened. We've got a dead man in the mortuary to prove it! And we've got a blood-stained piece of iron."

"And we've got a false beard," murmured the divisional inspector.

"And we've got a false beard!" agreed Mr. Budd. "And all we've got to do is to connect 'em up, You've got a man watchin' Thane?"

Hadlow nodded.

"Well, you'd better put another on to watch Tinsdale, and a third to keep an eye on this house and see that nobody tries to do a bunk," said Mr. Budd rapidly. "I don't know anythin' definite yet, but I'm not takin'

any chances. Maybe we're all wrong. Maybe that feller Thane is at the bottom of the business. Maybe his disembodied spirit came in through the window, bashed old Hayles on the head, and slipped out through the keyhole! Maybe he employed Isis or Thor, or some of his queer friends, and got a spook to pop that weight into Kathleen Travers' wardrobe. Maybe—" He stopped suddenly. "Maybe!" he ended in a peculiar voice.

"What have you thought of?" asked Hadlow.

The interview was taking place in the big main bedroom, and he stared thoughtfully at the foot of the bed.

"I don't know," he said slowly, and his energy slid from him like a cloak, leaving him sleepy and lethargic. "I dunno. I've got somethin' poppin' in my head."

He became so absent and distrait from that moment that the divisional inspector curtailed his visit.

"I shall be at the station if you want me," he said, as Mr. Budd accompanied him down the stairs.

"Maybe I will want you later," murmured the stout man thoughtfully. "If I can find the 'how', I shall certainly want you."

"The how and the why," said Hadlow; but the big man shook his head.

"I think I've found the why," he remarked. "Both the why and the who. Yes, I think I have. It's the how that's beating me. But maybe I'll find that, too."

They had reached the deserted hall, and Hadlow glanced at the big grandfather clock that was solemnly

ticking.

"Good lord, I'd no idea it was so late!" he declared. "I've got an appointment at seven, and it's nearly half-past six now. What's the matter?"

For Mr. Budd was staring at the clock as though he'd seen a ghost.

"Eh?" The stout man turned. "Eh? What did you say?"

"What were you staring at?" demanded the divisional inspector. "Did you see something?"

"Yes, I saw somethin'," agreed Mr. Budd, and there was a queer, excited note in his voice. "I saw somethin'. I think it's likely you'll be gettin' that telephone call, after all."

* * * * * * *

Sergeant Leek, having been left to his own devices, elected to go for a walk. It was warm and pleasant, and the country surrounding the Manor House was worth exploring. He strolled along leafy lanes and broad highways, through woods and across commons, a lean, melancholy figure in his rather shabby suit of blue serge.

In his own fashion he enjoyed himself, although no one seeing him would have imagined so for an instant. He had rather the appearance of having just left the funeral of some near and beloved relation. His long face wore an expression of settled melancholy, and his sad eyes surveyed the beauties around him without apparent enthusiasm.

He found a little teashop on the outskirts of Liddenhurst, and came back in the calm of the evening while the church bells were ringing, fervently hoping that Mr. Budd had not been requiring him. But when he reached the Manor House there was no sign of the big man. He was not in his bedroom, and he was not in the grounds. He appeared to have disappeared.

Dinner was over, for which the sergeant was thankful. These meals in which you all sat round the table and stared at one another embarrassed him. He liked eating alone and in comfort. He had brought in a packet of sandwiches, and, going to his room, he munched them comfortably.

It was funny where the 'sooper' had got to. Perhaps he'd gone down to the inn after beer. The sergeant strongly disapproved of alcoholic drink.

He finished his frugal meal, and picked up an old magazine, which he found in the room. He was still reading when at half-past nine the door opened and Mr. Budd came in.

"Where have you been to?" he demanded. "I've been lookin' for you everywhere."

"I didn't think you'd want me, so I went for a walk," answered Leek. "Was it anythin' important?"

"Oh, no!" said Mr. Budd sarcastically. "Just an inquiry into this murder."

"Well, I'd been 'angin' about all day," said the sergeant, "and nobody seemed to want me. Why didn't you say there might be somethin' doin'?"

"I was afraid it might interfere with your evenin's

enjoyment," said the stout superintendent. "I want you to find all the people stayin' in this house, with the exception of the servants, round 'em up in the drawin' room, and keep 'em there until I tell 'em they can go."

"What's up?" demanded Leek curiously.

"The balloon will be pretty soon!" said Mr. Budd complacently. "Now, get along downstairs and do as I tell you."

* * * * * * *

The divisional inspector was on the point of going home when the telephone call that Mr. Budd had suggested might possibly occur came through.

"I've got it all worked out," said the slow, sleepy voice. "If you'll come along up to the Manor House, I think I can show you how the impossible can be made possible."

"D'you mean you've discovered the how?" said Hadlow excitedly.

"I think I have," answered Mr. Budd. "Come along up."

The inspector was interested and lost no time. The call had come through at a quarter past ten, and at half-past he was talking to Mr. Budd in the latter's room.

"It's very simple," said the stout superintendent. "It was the clock that gave me the idea."

"The clock?" repeated Hadlow. "How in the world could that tell you? I don't see how a clock can explain a person making himself invisible."

"No, I don't suppose you do," said the superinten-

dent. "As a matter of fact, it doesn't. The person didn't make himself invisible."

"Then what did he do?" said the exasperated Hadlow. "If he wasn't invisible, somebody would have seen him."

"Anybody could have seen him," said Mr. Budd, a slight twinkle in his sleepy eyes.

"But nobody did see him," protested the baffled inspector. "You didn't see him and Sergeant Leek didn't see him."

"We didn't see him," explained the superintendent, "because we didn't look in the right place. If we'd looked in the right place, we should have seen him, all right. He didn't do anythin' supernatural. But he did do something that was remarkably clever."

Hadlow's patience was exhausted.

"Well, tell me," he said. "How did he get in and out of that room without being seen?"

"He didn't!" said the fat detective, with irritating calmness. "He didn't get in and out of that room without bein' seen for the very simple reason that he was never there!"

CHAPTER NINE
THE HOW AND THE WHY

The divisional inspector stared at the complacent Mr. Budd in stupefied bewilderment.

"But if he wasn't there," he protested, when he could find his voice, "how did he kill Hayles?"

"There you are, that's the clever part of it," said the stout man. "He not only killed Hayles, but he left his beard behind."

Hadlow made a gesture of despair.

"I give it up," he said.

"Well, I'll give you a practical demonstration," said Mr. Budd. "Come along to the study."

He took the inspector downstairs, turned into the corridor, and taking a key from his pocket unlocked the door of the room in which old Reuben Hayles had met his death. He reached for the switch.

"Now," he said, as the light came on, "take a look round. The place is exactly as it was last night."

Hadlow looked round keenly and discovered that the stout superintendent's words were true. With the exception of that sprawling figure on the rug, the room was exactly the same. Even the window had been

opened. He went over to it, and looked out. In contrast to the previous night, the sky was clear and the moon was just rising, a round yellow ball low on the horizon, rather like a gigantic Chinese lantern.

"Well," he said, "what next?" as Mr. Budd stood silently by and watched him.

"Next," said the fat detective, "I'm goin' to ask you to sit down on the edge of the bed there, and whatever happens you're not to move. Now listen very seriously to this, Hadlow. Whatever happens, don't move! If you do, you may get hurt."

"All right," promised the inspector. "I won't move. What are you going to do?" he asked in surprise, as his companion went ponderously to the door.

"I'm goin' to leave you for a minute or two," said Mr. Budd, "and by the time I come back you'll know just how Reuben Hayles died."

He disappeared, shutting the door behind him, and the bewildered Hadlow was left alone. He took his seat gingerly on the edge of the bed and stared about him, wondering what was going to happen next. There was something queerly uncomfortable about sitting in that lighted room in which a man had come by his death, waiting.

There was scarcely a sound in the house. The screech of an owl from outside came faintly to his ears, but nothing more. Dead silence!

He looked at the oblong patch that marked the window and instinctively he felt that the phenomenon he was about to witness would come from there. And

presently it did. Swiftly and without warning.

He heard the faintest rustle, and then a black object came hurtling through the open window—a silent, rushing missile.

With an exclamation, Hadlow half started to his feet, and then there was nothing. The window was blank once more.

The inspector's pent-up breath left his lips in a harsh sigh. He had seen, and yet he still didn't understand. The thing had come and gone with lightning speed. He was itching to go to that open window and look out, but he remembered Mr. Budd's words and remained where he was, stifling his curiosity and trying to curb his impatience.

A footstep sounded in the corridor, the handle turned softly, and the big man came into the room.

"Well," he said, "did you see it?"

"I saw it," said Hadlow. "What was it?"

"Three pounds of hard iron," answered Mr. Budd grimly. "The thing that struck Reuben Hayles and crushed the front of his skull like an eggshell."

"But what happened to it?" demanded Hadlow. "I still don't understand."

"Well, now come with me, and I'll show you the neatest murder machine that was ever conceived by the brain of man."

"Where are we going?" muttered the inspector.

"Upstairs again," said the stout superintendent,

Hadlow thought they were going back to his room, but he quickly discovered that this was not their desti-

nation. Mr. Budd paused before he reached it, opened a door on the right, and signed to his companion to enter. The inspector did so.

"Whose room is this?" he demanded.

"The room of the man who killed Hayles," said Mr. Budd, "It's immediately over his bedroom, as I expect you've guessed. Now look here."

He went over to the open window, and Hadlow saw, resting on the floor, the iron weight attached to a thin, strong wire.

"See that hook?" said Mr. Budd, pointing to a hook that had been screwed into the top of the window frame. "I put that there. He'd taken away the one he'd used last night, but the hole was there."

Still Hadlow didn't quite understand, although a glimmer was seeping into his brain.

"Don't you see?" said Mr. Budd. "Look at the oak tree."

"What's the oak tree got to do with it?" demanded the inspector,

"He fastened the weight to the end of the wire," explained the big man carefully, "and measured the wire so that when the other end was attached to this hook the weight hung down so that it was exactly level with the head of a man of the height of Reuben Hayles standing in the window below. And then he took a piece of twine, fastened that, too, to the weight, passed it over that branch of the oak tree, and brought the end of the twine back to the window of his room. Then he pulled the whole thing up out of sight among the

leaves. Got me?"

Hadlow nodded.

"All he had to do," went on Mr. Budd, "was to wait until the victim was standin' in the window below and cut the twine. The weight came rushin' down with almost the force of a bullet on the end of its wire, swung in through the open window, and hit Reuben Hayles a smashin' blow on the forehead. The force of the blow sent him staggering backwards, and he collapsed in the middle of the room. The weight, of course, immediately swung out again, and the man waitin' above pulled it quickly up. There was nothin' to be seen. Nothin' but a dead man in the room below, and no means to show how he'd been killed."

"Good lord! What a diabolical arrangement!" breathed Hadlow, and Mr. Budd nodded.

"Yes, it was diabolical and clever," he said.

"But," the inspector frowned, "how did he insure that Hayles would go to the window? He might not have gone near it, or the window might have been closed."

"He knew the window wouldn't be closed," said Mr. Budd. "I've been talkin' to Murley, and I understand that it was Mr. Hayles' habit to leave that window open day and night in all weathers. How he arranged for certain that Hayles would go to the window, is, I think, one of the cleverest touches of all. You remember the beard?"

Hadlow, who in the excitement had forgotten, stared.

"The beard?" repeated Mr. Budd. "The false beard.

He hung it on the end of a thread and dropped it down so that it would swing in the open window. Naturally, when Hayles came into the room and put on the light, and saw such an extraordinary thing danglin', he went over to examine it. He had it in his hand when the weight was released, and that's why it was there when we found him."

"But why a beard?" said Hadlow.

"Why not?" retorted Mr. Budd. "I think he had at the back of his mind an idea that he would clutch the beard and have it in his hand when he was found. It 'ud help to create the illusion which he wanted—that someone had actually been in the room and struck the blow."

"But when was all this arranged?" said the inspector. "It must have been prepared beforehand. He must have needed a ladder to get up the oak tree."

"Oh, yes!" said Mr. Budd. "It was all prepared beforehand. It was all waitin' there right through Saturday. But the wire and the thread were so fine that you couldn't see them unless you were lookin' for 'em. And who would expect to look for such a thing?"

"And who—who occupies this room?"

He looked round.

"The feller we're goin' down now to arrest," said Mr. Budd. "The fellow who planned not only one murder, but two. There was another one in his mind, but it wasn't goin' to look like murder. It was goin' to look like justice. The man who tried to frame Kathleen Travers by puttin' that weight in her wardrobe—Mr.

Geoffrey Dinwater!"

* * * * * * *

Mr. Budd sat in the Assistant-Commissioner's office on the Monday afternoon and listened with gratification to the words of praise which Colonel Blair had offered in connection with his efforts at Liddenhurst.

"The astounding thing to me," said the grey-haired, dapper man, "is that you cleared the whole thing up in such a short time. Excellent work, Superintendent—excellent!"

The big man's heavy face flushed faintly.

"I thought at one time I was goin' to fall down on it," he said. "And I believe I would have done if it hadn't been for the clock."

"The clock?" said the puzzled Assistant-Commissioner, who had heard nothing about a clock.

"There was a grandfather clock in the hall," explained Mr. Budd. "One of those big things with weights and a pendulum. I'd just found that three-pound weight, and was puzzlin' over the mystery of that room, when I saw the pendulum, and it gave me the idea."

"Dinwater, of course, was after the money," said Colonel Blair.

"Oh, yes!" answered the superintendent. "The money was at the back of it. When he confessed, after we'd cornered him and shown him exactly how he'd done the trick, he admitted that he'd got into a hell of a mess with moneylenders, and worse things, and didn't know which way to turn. Then his uncle showed him

one of them stupid letters from Thane, and he began to wonder if he couldn't use it as a cloak for his own ends."

"But the whole object was to implicate the girl," said the colonel.

"The object was general mystification and a good alibi for himself," corrected Mr. Budd. "The girl could be attended to after. With her out of the way he became next of kin, and naturally the money would have gone to him."

"But I don't see," protested the Assistant-Commissioner, frowning, "how be was going to get the girl out of the way. Until you discovered how the trick was worked, you couldn't have arrested her, and once you'd discovered that, it was obvious who'd done the murder."

"I don't think," said the big man slowly, and his face was grave, "that he was altogether relyin' on our arrestin' her. I've got an idea from somethin' he said that Kathleen Travers would have committed suicide, or so it would have appeared. And everybody would have thought she'd done it because she was guilty."

"Good heavens!" Colonel Blair stared. "You mean that Dinwater would have—"

"I think he would," broke in the superintendent, nodding. "He was a nasty piece of work—a very nasty piece of work! But he was clever—I will say that. It was one of the neatest ideas I've ever come across."

His fingers went mechanically to his waistcoat pocket, and he produced a cigar before he remembered

where he was. Rather embarrassed, he was putting it back when the Assistant-Commissioner stopped him.

"Smoke if you want to," he said generously, and with a sigh of content Mr. Budd stuck the cigar between his lips and felt in his pocket for his matches.

ABOUT THE AUTHOR

GERALD VERNER (1897-1980) was born John Robert Stuart Pringle in London on 31 January 1897, He was one of the most prolific and successful British writers of detective thrillers. His earliest novels, beginning in the late 1920s, were issued under the pen name of Donald Stuart, particularly his numerous "Sexton Blake" stories. His first novel as Gerald Verner. *THE EMBANKMENT MURDER*, appeared in 1933, and thereafter Verner became his adopted name, and was used for most of his work, although he continued to write occasionally as Stuart, also adding two other successful pen names, Derwent Steele and Nigel Vane. He published more than 120 novels, and was translated into over 35 languages. Many of his books were adapted into radio serials, stage plays, and films. He also wrote television serials, and one of his original screenplays, *DOUBLE DANGER*, was used for a 1961 episode of *THE AVENGERS*.

One of his most successful characters was Mr. Robert Budd, a Detective Superintendent of the C.I.D. Rather portly, deceptively sleepy-eyed, and seemingly a plodder, Mr. Budd was actually razor-sharp, and

solved cases as well as any slick private detective of fiction. He was aided, rather unwillingly at times, by the melancholy and slower-witted Sergeant Leek, the butt of Mr. Budd's biting sarcasm.

Verner's work was frequently compared to that of Edgar Wallace, and he was noted for his exciting, fast-action plots, some of them recognised as classics of the locked-room and "impossible crime" genres.